Life

Elise Noble

Published by Undercover Publishing Limited

ISBN: 978-1-910954-44-7

Edited by Nikki Mentges, NAM Editorial

Cover art by Abigail Sins

www.undercover-publishing.com

www.elise-noble.com

To the lovely folks of Southwinds Coffee, for providing plenty of inspiration for this book.

CHAPTER 1

RAIN SOAKED MY hair as I half walked, half ran from the Tube station to the church hall. *Mental note: next week, bring trainers and don't wear a pencil skirt.* Puddles and LK Bennett heels didn't make good playmates.

I glanced at my watch. Five minutes late, but it was a miracle I'd made it at all. Milton Berkeley, head partner at the law firm of Berkeley, Rogers and Smyth, where I'd worked since graduating from Oxford University, didn't take too kindly to me leaving the office at seven thirty every Thursday, never mind the other sixty hours I always worked over the week.

I could still hear his nasal voice echoing in my head. "Leaving early again, Catherine?"

But just over seven months ago, on a chilly New Year's Eve, I'd promised myself that I'd take one evening a week to do something other than work. Just one. A hundred and twenty minutes to spend as I pleased.

Full of enthusiasm and Christmas pudding, I'd signed up for an aerobics class to start with, but the rows of perfectly coordinated, Lycra-clad ladies had looked at me with such disdain I'd shed tears when I'd got home. Yes, I knew I needed to lose a few pounds, but having hips was hardly a crime, was it? Anyway, on week four, when I stopped at the all-night convenience store to buy a chocolate bar to cheer myself up on the way back to my flat, I'd spotted a flyer on the counter.

Art classes.

I'd always enjoyed art at school. When I was a child, I'd wanted to be a painter, although my mother had been less than enthusiastic about the masterpiece I'd created on the living room wall when the nanny fell asleep on the sofa. And my father? When the time came for me to go to university, he decreed that I should study for a "proper" career if I wanted his help with tuition fees.

So...art. The next morning, I'd shoved all my designer workout gear to the back of my wardrobe and bought myself a whole selection of pens, pencils, paper, and paint on the internet before I went to the office.

Fast forward to July, and holding a brush to canvas rather than a Biro to a legal pad for two hours each week was the only thing that kept me going. Thursday evenings had become my lifeline.

Tonight, water dripped off me as I pushed through the double doors and stumbled over to the only empty seat in the room. Why were there so many people here? Usually, the class was half-empty, only five or six students, but today there were eleven others. I scanned the room and realised there was actually one more vacant seat—a solitary stool sat in the centre of a raised dais, and that was where many of my fellow attendees were focusing.

"Never heard of an umbrella?" Marie whispered as I collapsed onto the chair she'd saved for me. Another benefit of art classes—I'd made a friend, my only one outside of work.

"I forgot it, and there were no cabs. Are we supposed to be drawing the stool?"

"You missed the announcement last week. We're doing five sessions of life drawing."

Ah yes, last week. Mr. Berkeley had caught me as I was leaving and insisted I spend two hours going over the strategy for his court appearance the next day. It was the first time I'd skipped an art class, and when I got home, I'd drunk half a bottle of red wine while I threw darts at a photo of the grumpy old coot to bolster my spirits. The dartboard had been an impulse purchase from eBay one lunchtime, or as I preferred to call it, an investment in my sanity.

"So, where's the model?" I asked Marie.

"Delores went to help him get ready."

Him? At school, we'd drawn a woman, one who looked like she'd rather have been anywhere but posing for a class of sixth-form students, and I'd captured the scowl on her face perfectly if I said so myself. But Delores, our teacher, had picked a man? Hmm, I liked her more and more. After all, since Mr. Berkeley banned us from having desktop calendars featuring shirtless models, I rarely got the chance to admire the male physique, and my working hours didn't give me time to date.

Okay, so if I was honest, the idea of actually dating again terrified me.

My last attempt ended in failure over a year ago, when the accountant I'd been seeing for eight months sent me a text message saying I was too boring and he thought we should see other people. Boring? Coming from a man who collected antique calculators, that really, really stung, but the internet came to the rescue once again with express delivery of a Rampant Rabbit and an economy-sized box of chocolate caramels.

"Him?" I muttered out loud, and Marie grinned.

"Why do you think there are so many people here tonight? Last year, Delores came up with an off-duty fireman. Week one, he posed in his uniform, and week two, he whipped everything off. We almost had to call his friends at the station to come and hose us down."

I fished my sketchbook out of my bag, cursing under my breath at the damp edges. At least I hadn't worn mascara today, or I'd have had that mess to contend with as well. I was just getting my pencils out when Delores swished in. Today's muumuu was sparkly green, and it matched her eyeshadow perfectly. An older lady, she exuded the sort of confidence I'd only ever dreamed of. Even now, seven years into my legal career, I still felt sick every time I stepped through the doors of a courtroom.

"Ladies and gentleman." Delores glanced over at Miguel, the sole male in the room. "We've got a treat tonight. The lovely Joe is going to model for us."

She beckoned to someone behind us, and jaws dropped as Joe ambled to the front of the class, wearing only a sheet around his waist. He perched on the stool while Delores arranged the fabric to cover the good bits, and then he followed her directions to, "Lean forward a bit. Move your hand."

Beside me, Marie's pencil rolled out of her fingers and under Miguel's chair, and it took him a second or two to snap his eyes away from Joe and retrieve it for her.

Finally happy with Joe's pose, Delores clapped her hands. "This evening, we're going to practise our sketching. Joe's going to move every twenty minutes, which will give you the chance to explore various positions."

From the way the other girls were salivating, I knew exactly which positions they wanted to explore. Even Marie, who had a boyfriend. I reached over and tapped her pad.

"We're supposed to be drawing."

"I'm committing his muscles to memory before I start. Wonder what would happen if I visited the ladies' room and accidentally tripped over that sheet?"

With Marie, I could never quite tell if she was serious. This was the woman who'd once scrambled over a screaming crowd to clamber on stage with Justin Timberlake and managed to squeeze his ass before security hauled her away. I knew because she showed me the video on her phone. Loosening Joe's sheet would be nothing for Marie.

A low hum of chatter started as I measured out rough proportions and studied Joe's limbs. How long did he spend in the gym to get those thigh muscles? Despite what I'd said to Marie, it was a minute or two before I put pencil to paper myself. Doing justice to the man who'd stepped right out of my dirtiest daydreams suddenly became the most important thing in my life. My fingers shook a little as I sketched the outline of his body and began filling in the details of his face. The strong nose. The little smile that played across his lips as he stared at the wall to the side of me. What was he thinking about? The harsh lighting in the hall played off the planes of his face as he moved an inch.

It seemed like no time at all had passed before Delores posed him again, only this time he was looking straight at me. For a second, our gazes locked, his blue eyes on my brown ones, and my heart raced, threatening to hammer its way out of my ribcage. Was it possible to have a lust-induced heart attack? Visions of me getting carted off in an ambulance flashed through my mind, but still I couldn't tear my eyes away. In the end, it was Joe who broke the connection, moving those grey-flecked irises higher so he was looking over my head.

"That man's gonna set my lady bits on fire," Marie muttered.

"What about Andy? You know, your dearly beloved?" At least for the past six weeks.

"I adore Andy, of course I do, but no woman with a pulse could sit here with dry knickers."

Wasn't that the truth? I shifted uncomfortably on my chair, all too aware of my own damp patch.

"Come on, tell me that's true," Marie prodded.

"Some of us have self-control," I hissed, then immediately wished I'd kept my voice down, because Joe's eyes lowered to meet mine again. This time, Delores saved me as she peered over my shoulders and pointed at Joe's pencilled waist.

"You've got your proportions slightly wrong there. His torso needs to be longer." She pointed in his direction, and I was forced to count his abs. "See?"

"Yes, I see." Eight-pack, not six-pack.

"I'll move Joe in a moment, and you can have another go."

Almost halfway through the class, and the thought of walking out and never seeing Joe again brought me out in a cold sweat. Not that I was anywhere near his league—Joe was Olympic gold, while I was more last-in-the-egg-and-spoon-race—but the chance to openly and legitimately admire someone that gorgeous didn't come along often.

"Are we using the same model for all the life drawing classes?" I asked.

Delores didn't bother to hide her smile. "Ooh, yes. Much better for your development that way, don't you think?"

"Definitely."

Beside me, Marie was grinning too as Delores headed for the dais.

"Four more weeks of that," Marie said. "These art classes are worth every penny."

Miguel overheard her and licked his lips. "I'd pay double."

"Triple if he took the sheet away."

"Guys, you can't keep talking about him like he's a piece of meat," I told them. "He's only here to model."

"So you're telling me you wouldn't...you know...?"

"I'm focused on my career. I don't have time to date."

"Who said anything about dating? A good shag might stop you from being so uptight."

"I'm not uptight," I snapped.

Marie giggled. "Whatever you say."

Glancing across the room, I caught a slim girl with blonde hair raising her phone to take a quick photo of Joe while he wasn't looking, and I wished I were brave enough to do the same thing. Knowing my luck, he'd catch me just as I clicked the shutter, which would necessitate dying of embarrassment and thus not being able to return to class for the next month. Maybe on week five...

"Don't forget to draw, ladies," Delores said. "And you, Miguel."

Ah yes, the drawing. I picked up my pencil again, thankful that this time Joe was facing away from me, and carried on with my mission to commit every part of him to both memory and paper before the end of his sessions. The way a lock of his tousled blond hair fell over his forehead. His square jaw, clean-shaven, with that little cleft in his chin crying out to be licked. *Stop it, Cate!* But I couldn't. I spent more time looking than drawing, but I stayed away from his eyes. Those eyes were dangerous to a girl's heart. I shifted my gaze to his body instead and allowed myself to drink in the detail of the tattoo on his upper arm. A skull with a snake twined through its empty eye sockets, a little creepy, but it gave Joe an edge that only made him sexier. As did the faint scar on his thigh, a starburst of pale flesh. How had he got that?

His lips quirked up for a second, as did my pulse rate. What was going through his mind? The bunch of horny women drooling over him? Or something more mundane, like pizza or football?

The final hour passed all too quickly, and it was time to pack up.

"Good thing I'm getting my hair done before next week," Marie said.

"Andy?" I reminded her again.

"What's wrong with a girl wanting to look her best?"

"Or a guy," Miguel chipped in. "You never know, he might be on the other team."

A groan escaped my lips before I could help myself, and Marie turned to face me.

"I knew it! You *are* interested."

"Not at all. I merely remembered I'd forgotten to book myself in for a trim. It's been on my to-do list for weeks."

I wasn't entirely lying. It was just that getting my hair cut usually rated somewhere near the bottom of my list of priorities. At work, I could fasten it back in a bun and nobody knew the difference.

Marie and Miguel exchanged knowing smiles, and Marie nodded.

"Sure, I believe you."

I finished shoving my pencils into my bag, looking up in time to catch one last glimpse of Joe as he walked out to get dressed. The next six days and twenty-two hours would be the slowest of my life.

CHAPTER 2

"CATHERINE, WHAT ARE you doing over there? I needed those papers twenty minutes ago."

Crappity crap. What *was* I doing? Oh, that's right, staring at all those little words on my computer screen but only seeing Joe's face. I'd figured the whole Joe-fantasy thing was safe enough, seeing as nobody else could see what was running through my grubby mind, but now I realised I'd have to be more careful.

"Two minutes, Mr. Berkeley. I'll just print them out."

Oh, the joys of being a lawyer. When I'd told my father I'd be studying law at Oxford, he'd been over the moon, and for five long years he'd expected me to follow in his footsteps as a barrister. I tried, really I did, and I even defended a couple of cases once I'd passed the bar exam, but the whole arguing-in-front-of-people thing brought me out in hives. Literally. Big red blotches, and the doctor said it was due to stress. I'd switched to property law instead, much to my family's disappointment, which meant I got the joys of dealing with overhanging trees and boundary disputes, but at least I rarely needed to stand before a judge.

I quickly read over the letter on screen one more time. Our client was arguing with his next-door neighbour about the position of her new fence. Neither side would back down over what amounted to four inches of scrubby grass. Four inches! Even my ex, Mr. Calculator, had a longer dick than that—barely—and from the look of the photos, neither of the parties involved liked gardening, anyway. But the client was paying our fees, so who was I to question it?

Mr. Berkeley took the papers with a scowl and I backed out of his office, raising an eyebrow at his PA. What put him in such a happy mood this Friday?

"He forgot his wife's birthday," she whispered. "Mrs. B yelled at him so loud one of the neighbours called the police."

"Ouch."

"She's making him take her away for the weekend, which means he's had to cancel his golf game and three meetings this afternoon."

"Does that mean we don't need to go through the Walker files tomorrow?"

She grimaced apologetically. "Uh, it means *you* need to go through the Walker files tomorrow."

Terrific. "It's not like I wanted Saturday off, anyway."

If Mr. Berkeley was leaving early and expected me to do his work, then I was damn well doing it at home rather than in the office. And maybe, just maybe, I could stop off and get my hair cut on my way home. Not because I'd be seeing Joe again in less than a week. Not in the slightest. Okay, perhaps there was a tiny part that felt I should make the effort. After all, I got to look at his delicious body for two whole hours, so the least I could do was get rid of my split ends. And possibly wear make-up. And lose ten pounds. Or thirty.

Cate! Enough!

Less than twenty-four hours had passed since I'd first laid eyes on the man, and already he was consuming my every waking thought. And my sleeping ones too if last night was anything to go by.

Which was perhaps why I woke up early on Saturday and dug the dreaded Lycra out of the bottom of my wardrobe. When I'd bought my flat in Heron Court six months ago, one of the attractions had been the residents' gym. No more aerobics classes full of yummy mummies and fitness fanatics—I could burn a few calories without having to leave my own building and pick a time when nobody else was around to do it.

Was it me, or did the leggings feel tighter than last time I wore them? I glanced at the roll of stomach sticking over the waistband and sucked it in. Nope, not much improvement. I definitely needed to cut down on the calories.

I'd always been a comfort eater, ever since my mother forced me to take gymnastics classes at the age of seven—flexible and coordinated I was not—but lately at work, with all those hours spent at my desk... Well, they hadn't been kind to my thighs, had they?

Six thirty, and I shuffled down to the basement. We even had a pool, not that I'd ever use it. The treadmill I could just about handle, but a swimsuit? No way.

I plugged in my headphones and hopped onto a stationary bike, then fiddled with the controls until I felt the resistance. Fifteen minutes. I'd start with fifteen minutes and work up. Joe was at the forefront of my thoughts as I pedalled, and this time I didn't bother to push him away. Hell, I deserved some sort of reward for all this sweat. And I wasn't doing the exercise for him, exactly, more using him as inspiration to get a little fitter, because the man clearly worked out.

Except my daydreams were interrupted after ten minutes by the door opening, letting in a waft of warm air from the corridor outside.

"Morning."

The newcomer raised his hand in greeting, and I recognised the guy who lived next to me on the third floor. We'd barely said more than "hello" in the corridor, although he had left me a fruit basket as a welcome gift. Now he was closer, I took the opportunity to have a better look. Light brown hair, matching eyes, and an athletic physique. Not bad, but not a patch on Joe.

"Hi, er..." Too late, I realised I didn't know his name.

"Dane."

"Hi, Dane."

He stared at me expectantly.

"Oh, yes, uh, I'm Cate."

Idiot Cate, who couldn't even say hello to a stranger without tripping over my own tongue. My mouth had as much coordination as my feet most of the time, which was another reason I liked art classes with Joe. While I drew, he was the silent type.

I figured Dane would do his own thing and give up on trying to have a conversation, but he sat on the bike next to me instead.

"I haven't seen you in here before?" he said.

"First time." A nervous giggle escaped.

"Everybody has to start somewhere. Do you know how all the equipment works?"

"I can work it out, thanks."

He acted like he hadn't heard as he leaned over the

front of my bike. "Look, it's easy. You can toggle between distance and calories on the display, see?"

"Really, it's fine. I don't need help."

Only when I switched to the rowing machine, there he was again, fiddling with the foot plates while I tried to adjust the straps over my shoes. I gritted my teeth as he declared everything "just right." After all, he was only trying to be nice, and most people in Heron Court had ignored me since I moved in. Maybe I should have made more effort to introduce myself, but talking to new people made me so nervous I didn't know where to start.

Dane didn't seem to have that problem.

"So, you moved in a few months ago, right?"

"Yes."

"Have you always lived in London, or was it a big relocation?"

"Apart from my years at uni, yes, I've always lived here, but I was renting before."

Dane let out a low whistle. "You *bought* your apartment here? On your own?"

"It took a while before I could afford it, but I always wanted my own place. Not many rental properties allow cats."

And those that did usually jacked up the price and demanded an obscene security deposit, which was why I'd spent almost six years living in shoddy flats while I'd saved every penny. Property law might have been dull, but it paid well, and when I became the youngest ever junior partner at Berkeley, Rogers and Smyth, I'd celebrated with my extravagant purchase. Two of my goals in life achieved, even if Mr. Berkeley did still treat me like a glorified secretary on occasion. At least the rest of my colleagues weren't as bad. Okay, they were, but I was good at my job.

"You've got cats?" Dane asked.

"Two. Thor and Loki."

"Ah, so you also have an interest in Norse mythology?"

"Uh, yes." It was better than admitting I had an interest in Chris Hemsworth and Tom Hiddleston. "Something like that."

Come to think of it, Joe did bear more than a passing resemblance to Chris. Perhaps that was why I couldn't get him out of my more than slightly obsessed mind.

"I was always into Roman history myself. You know, the architecture and the engineering. We wouldn't be half the society we are today if it wasn't for the Romans."

"I'm sure."

He began droning on about the merits of a hypocaust heating system while I blocked out the sound of his voice. Men rarely paid me any attention, but now a miracle had happened and one finally had, I wished more than anything that he'd leave me alone.

I'd planned to finish off with a walk on the treadmill, but when I headed in that direction Dane did too, so I veered towards the door. I could walk to the shops later instead. I was almost out of chocolate. No, fruit. I was almost out of fruit. Okay, wine.

"Finished already?" Dane asked.

"Yes, I've got a busy day ahead."

"Maybe I'll see you tomorrow?"

"Maybe." I managed a wave, already planning to shift my gym session to mid-morning to avoid any possibility of that happening.

***

Back in my apartment, the cats were waiting for breakfast. Thor, the Siberian, wove in and out of my legs as I walked in the door while Loki, the seal point Siamese, mewed from the arm of the sofa. Okay, so I was a few minutes later with breakfast than on a weekday, but he didn't need to make quite so much noise. At least the walls were reasonably thick at Heron Court. In our last place, the old biddy next door had complained if the cats so much as purred. Here, I could still hear Dane's television from time to time, and the woman below had a vacuuming fetish, but at least it didn't feel like we were in the same room.

On the whole, both cats were well behaved. Neither had experienced the best start in life, so I tended to spoil them a tiny bit. The accountant hadn't liked that either. His muttered comments about their deluxe kitty cabin and sparkly collars hadn't gone unnoticed.

Where other women in the office had photos of their husbands and kids propped up on their desks, Thor and Loki graced mine. Mr. Berkeley may have insisted on calling me Catherine rather than Cate, but the associates all called me crazy cat lady behind my back. Although I considered a woman needed at least three felines to achieve that status, I couldn't see myself losing the nickname anytime soon.

Perhaps I could take in a photo of Joe and prop it next to my computer? Head only, of course, or Mr. Berkeley would hit the roof. The mere thought had me choking on a mouthful of the orange juice I'd just poured. Everyone would see straight through the lie. Why? Because girls like me didn't date men like Joe.

CHAPTER 3

THURSDAY CAME FASTER than I thought, mainly because I barely stopped working, and my enthusiasm at seeing Joe was tempered with anxiety. Not over my art class—I felt perfectly safe there—but because I'd finally found the inspiration to start exercising and every single time I'd gone to use the gym, Dane had turned up too. He hadn't *done* anything beyond being slightly irritating and overly helpful, but in a windowless basement, his very presence gave me the creeps.

This morning, I'd given in to my discomfort and gone for a walk instead, only for him to catch up to me halfway across the local park and offer to buy me coffee.

"I'm in the middle of a walk."

"There's a Starbucks on the corner near our building. We can stop off on the way back."

"I'm late for work."

"Another time, then." Not a question, a statement.

"I work a lot."

"I've noticed that. What do you do?"

He'd been watching me? I suppressed a shudder. "I'm a lawyer."

I didn't want him to know anything about me, but I couldn't get myself out of the situation without appearing impolite.

Dane held up two crossed fingers in a mock "keep away" gesture, then laughed. "Well, I guess not all lawyers are that bad. Not one of those ambulance chasers, are you?"

With hindsight, I should have said I was. That I hung around waiting for innocent citizens to have an accident, trip, or fall so I could screw cash out of everybody concerned. But what came out was, "I work on property cases."

"Ah, well, I guess we can't all have interesting jobs."

"What do you do?"

"Recruitment consultant."

Oh, and they were so much more reputable than lawyers. At least we had an ethics code to stick to, and we didn't tend to stalk neighbours in our spare time. Speaking of spare time...

"Really? Which firm do you work for?"

"DB Consulting. My own firm. I run it from home."

Marvellous. I wasn't even safe in normal office hours.

He was still matching me step for step with an expectant expression, like I was supposed to be impressed by his stellar choice of profession, so I made a big show of looking at my watch. "Well, I'd better get going. I don't want to keep you from...whatever."

"You're not keeping me. We can walk back together. Are you going to build up to jogging soon?"

No, I was going to run. In the opposite direction. As fast as possible. But sadly, my thighs were already complaining about the amount of exercise I'd done this week, and my fledgling stamina wasn't up to a wild sprint. Instead, I marched off, eyes fixed ahead of me, and ignored Dane all the way back home. Even then he sprang ahead to hold the door open for me.

"I'll see you tomorrow," he said.

I sincerely hoped not. "Perhaps."

And perhaps I could camp out in the office. We had a microwave and a shower and a couple of pull-out beds for emergencies. And a security guard on the front desk who would keep out any strange men who happened to have an exercise fetish.

***

After I'd showered and fed the cats, I quickly ran the vacuum cleaner around. I'd been using a new brand of cat litter and they'd been dropping gritty bits all over the flat, everywhere from the kitchen island to the sofa to my bed. The joys of sharing my home with two felines who did as they pleased. Chores done, I hurried out the door and almost tripped over the Starbucks cup in the hallway. What the hell? The accompanying note made me seethe when I unfolded it.

Kate,
Roses are red,
This coffee's for you,
When I'm not by your side,
I feel so blue.

Oh, good grief. Now he was sending me terrible poems. He couldn't even spell my name right. Look on the bright side—at least that meant he hadn't been going through my mail. I flipped the lid off the coffee, and the sickly sweet smell of a caramel macchiato wafted up at me, complete with an unhealthy dollop of whipped cream. Not good for my diet or my teeth. I was an espresso girl, the stronger the better. I took a few seconds to pour the sugary mess down the sink before I ran out of the door. Even Thor and Loki looked at it with disgust.

Now I really was late for work. The four-inch property dispute was going to mediation this morning, and I was expected to attend, but I had a horrible feeling that one would go to the wire. What else would they do? Settle for two inches each? Gut instinct told me the argument was due to more than a simple fence-line issue, but my client didn't care to enlighten me on the details, and when I'd tactfully suggested to him that it might help if I had all the facts, he'd snapped back that it was none of my business.

But at least I had my art bag and my umbrella with me.

In the kitchenette on my floor, the gossip was already in full flow by the time I tiptoed past to the coffee machine. Sonia from corporate led the charge as she usually did. She may have been the firm's best negotiator, but she was also its worst bitch.

"...And I saw Linda out with the window cleaner last week. I know he's got a nice ass, but really? A window cleaner?"

Becky, the office slut, piped up. "Hey, I pulled one of those guys at the car wash the other day. He didn't speak a word of English, but he sure knew what to do in the bedroom."

Sonia rolled her eyes. "But you weren't *dating* him."

"How do you know Linda's dating the window cleaner?"

"They were having pizza in the place down the street, and Susie said they were sitting reeeeally close."

I pushed the button for a double espresso as Sally from accounts joined the party. "At least he was buying her dinner. He did get the bill, right?"

Despite the posh outfits and six-figure salaries, sometimes it felt like being back in the schoolyard again.

I grabbed a banana from the fruit bowl rather than my usual Danish pastry and slunk off back to my desk. Normally, I didn't mind work—indeed, since I graduated I'd thrived on it—but today the eleven hours I spent at my desk dragged as I watched the clock on my computer screen tick through the day.

Marie's mid-morning text message did nothing to quell my nerves: *Reckon Delores will whip Joe's sheet off tonight?*

Me: I kind of hope not - I won't get any painting done.

Marie: Don't be so serious. You can paint fruit or something tomorrow. Tonight is all about our viewing pleasure.

Fruit? Right. I glanced over at the banana still sitting on my desk and tried to erase that thought from my mind.

In the afternoon, I got the joy of my client calling the mediator an arsehole before he stormed out, and Mr. Berkeley's face turned an alarming shade of puce when I told him about it. But then he rubbed his hands together and smiled. "At least we can bill them for court costs now."

Hurrah.

Seven thirty came, and my run of bad luck continued on the Tube. The man next to me clutched the overhead rail, which put my nose level with his armpit, and he didn't know how to use deodorant. I tried to shuffle down a bit, but the sniffles of the woman on the other side and an inability to cover her mouth when she coughed soon sent me back again. Four stops, three stops, two, one. I practically ran off the train and out of the station. Only my aching legs stopped me from sprinting up the stairs. Although I felt better for having done a little exercise, my muscles, so unused to any kind of physical activity, tended to stiffen up in the day as I sat at my desk.

But then I was at the church hall, and Marie grinned as she patted the empty seat next to her. Primo position, front and centre. She must have got there first.

"Should have brought popcorn instead of pencils this week," she said. "Face it, I'm not planning to draw much."

"You don't like the challenge?"

"What challenge? Trying not to drool? No, I prefer to give Joe's abs my full attention."

"What about Andy?"

"Hey, I sat through the whole of that new film with him at the cinema last night. You know, the one with the swimsuit model. What's her name?"

"Uh, I'm not sure." I never went to the cinema. I didn't have the time or the inclination to go on my own. "Kate Upton?"

"No, not her. It doesn't matter. There was literally no plot, no hot guys, and she didn't wear many clothes either. I deserve this."

"When you put it that way, I can't argue." I leaned forward to get my sketchbook from my bag and winced as my ass muscles seized. "Ouch."

"What's wrong?"

"I finally started using the gym this week, and now I understand why I love my sofa so much."

Marie glanced over at the empty dais, and then her eyes widened as she put two and two together and made sixty-nine. "OMG. You like him."

"Who?"

"Don't play dumb. You know perfectly well who I'm talking about."

Of course I did, but I waved a hand in feigned nonchalance. "No, not at all. I've been meaning to go down to the gym since I moved in, and this week I finally got around to it."

"So it's absolutely nothing to do with an incredibly hot man who obviously spends a lot of time lifting weights."

"No, and besides, I'm probably going to quit exercising."

"Why? Are you that sore?"

I shook my head. "Nothing a packet of ibuprofen won't cure. But I seem to have attracted the attention of a slight weirdo." Her eyebrows rose as I described Dane's exploits, finishing with his coffee delivery this morning.

"Most girls would like a man who wrote them poetry."

"Most girls would like a man who didn't watch their every move and then invite themselves on a morning jog."

"He does seem slightly odd, I'll give you that. But is he good looking?"

I rolled my eyes. "Do you ever think of anything but a tight ass and a six-pack?"

"Good teeth are important."

Did Joe have good teeth? I'd never seen them, or heard him talk, for that matter. He could have had a voice like a schoolgirl and dentures for all I knew. I found myself staring at his jaw as he walked in behind Delores, who'd dressed up for the occasion again in a frilly pink muumuu and matching headscarf. Even her nail polish was colour coordinated.

As Joe passed me, he caught my eye. I quickly looked away. Dammit. Why did I always retreat into my insecurities? When I found the courage to look up again, I was just in time to see Delores tug his sheet away, revealing two round globes of a perfect ass. The gasp that went around the packed class said I wasn't the only person to think that way. Miguel even licked his lips.

Delores arranged Joe so he was sitting on one cheek, left leg out to the side as he leaned on his right hand.

Oh, I knew this life drawing class was a bad idea. How were we supposed to concentrate on drawing with...with *that* in front of us? The only thing more distracting would be the front view. Good grief, Delores had that planned for next week, didn't she? I'd have to bring a bloody towel to sit on.

I finally managed to bring my heart rate down enough to sketch an outline, and I noticed that all Marie had managed to do so far was doodle a heart in the corner of the page. When she caught me checking her work, she sighed and began with Joe's buttocks.

"That man's wasted here," she whispered. "He should be doing calendars. Like, all the months."

She was absolutely right, but all I could do was

carry on with my poor imitation of the real thing. Maybe I should invest in a lapel camera? That way I could record the sessions for posterity and play them over when I needed a pick-me-up. I'd even skip the chocolate caramels in favour of a little eye candy.

Once I got going, I found the drawing was actually a bit easier this week because I couldn't see his face. There was no risk of accidentally getting lost in those blue eyes, or worse, him catching me doing it. And that ass... I fanned myself unconsciously, and of course Marie noticed and got the giggles.

"Are you going to draw the rest of him?" I asked.

Joe's buttocks were now beautifully shaded, and she'd started on a second pair, in charcoal rather than pencil this time.

"Nah. I come here to enjoy myself, and I am. Just hope we get the front view next week. I'd give sculpting a try for that."

"You're incorrigible."

"You wouldn't want me any other way, and because you're my friend, I'm gonna gift you one of these lovely pictures at the end of class."

I couldn't help laughing as I offered her my pencil. "In that case, you carry on."

By the time class finished, I had one reasonably good drawing of Joe plus two of his backside—one from Marie, and I might have had a quick go myself. Purely for artistic reasons, you understand.

When Delores handed him back the sheet at ten o'clock, I bit back a groan. How was I supposed to go back to drawing inanimate objects after this? As Joe walked off to change, he went right past me, close enough that I could have reached out to touch him if I hadn't been sitting on my hands. And when he was two feet away, he smiled. Freaking smiled. At me. I know because I checked just in case there was somebody standing behind, but there wasn't. He didn't show any teeth, but there was a definite curve to his lips, and it made my entire body tingle as my skin flushed from my toes to the tips of my ears.

The man was so damn sexy, and if I compared future potential suitors against him, I knew one thing for sure: they'd all be found wanting.

CHAPTER 4

AFTER SPENDING AN entire evening staring at Joe, I was inspired enough to get up at half past five in the morning to use the gym. I thought I'd got away with it until Dane stumbled in at ten to six looking less than his usual dapper self. His T-shirt was rumpled, and a label hung out the back of his shorts.

"Early today," he mumbled.

"You didn't have to get up and join me."

"Wouldn't want my favourite girl to get lonely, now would I?"

"Sometimes I like being on my own. It gives me time to think."

He swung a leg over the saddle of the bike next to me and cranked the pedals. "You spend every evening alone in your apartment." When he reached out and patted my hand, I almost slapped his away. "A pretty girl like you should have a man in her life."

I took a deep breath and went for it. "Dane, I'm just not sure you're that man."

His face crumpled, his feet slowed, and for a moment I thought he was going to leave. But my celebrations were short lived when he mustered up a smile.

"I can see I have work left to do. How about dinner? I'll take you out somewhere fancy. What kind of food do you prefer? I bet you're a dessert girl, right? Something sweet, just like you."

Please, enough already. "Sorry, but I'm just not sure that would work."

His smile grew wider and he nodded to himself. "Yes, I definitely still have work left to do. But don't worry, I'm not giving up. From the moment I first saw you, I knew you were the girl for me, but it took me a while to work out you were single. Then you started using the gym, and it was like an omen. You see?"

No. No, I didn't see. "How is my wish to get fitter an omen?"

He spread his arms wide, still pedalling. "Nobody else uses this place except Ron from the second floor, and he always goes at lunchtime. Crazy, isn't it? All the other residents are too old or too busy. I've had it to myself the whole year, and now you're here with me."

When he put it like that, it wasn't so much an omen as a flipping nightmare, and he wasn't done.

"And then you walked past right in front of me on the morning I decided to go for a jog. It's like we were meant to be together."

Dammit, why did I decide to head outside yesterday?

"I'm not sure fate works like that."

"Neither was I, but now I'm convinced."

Okay, that was it. No more gym at Heron Court, at least while Dane was living there. He did say he was renting, right? I'd keep my fingers crossed for a collapse in the recruitment market, but meanwhile, I needed to find some other way of keeping fit. Maybe one of those exercise DVDs? I had two spare bedrooms, well, technically only one of them contained a bed—the other was completely empty. I could put a yoga mat in there, and then I wouldn't have to worry about horrifying the public with my jiggling thighs.

With that plan in mind, I muttered goodbye to Dane and practically ran out of the gym. eBay was calling my credit card's name.

**

By the time I finished drying my hair, I'd managed to purchase six different workout DVDs and a set of multi-coloured resistance bands, and I'd dug the yoga mat I never used out from the depths of the wardrobe. I was feeling pretty good about things until I saw the coffee and croissant Dane had left on the doorstep, together with a yellow post-it note stuck on the cup.

Cate,
Roses are red,
Sugar is sweet,
I hope one day,
You'll fall at my feet.

The poem was predictably awful, but that wasn't what made me stiffen. He'd spelled my name right. Cate with a C. How did he know? *Had* he been through my mail? We each had a locked box downstairs, but maybe he'd fished an envelope out of the slot or something? The thought made me shudder, and the high I'd felt from seeing Joe yesterday quickly evaporated as I scurried down the corridor. Dane's front door was at the far end, giving him a view to the lift if he looked out of his peephole. Was he watching? Was that how he always knew when I went to the gym? The pull-out bed in the break area at work looked more attractive by the second.

At least until I actually got to the break area and found Sonia relaxing on the sofa with a Danish and a cappuccino. Two years older than me, she'd bitched like hell when I made partner and she didn't, yet she never seemed to do any work. Theoretically, she assisted with our large corporate clients and tricky negotiations, but seemed to spend most of her time on Facebook. Or gossiping.

Apparently, this week Linda had been seen out for Saturday brunch with a headhunter for a rival firm, and nobody was sure whether she was looking for a new job or a roll in the sack. I'd be a little jealous if it was the former. Okay, also if it was the latter. It had been a long dry spell. Perhaps that was why Joe got to me so much? If I lowered my expectations a tad to, say, Dane, perhaps I wouldn't be consumed by thoughts of a certain tall, muscular blond every second of my life. But then again, I'd rather bathe in hornets than have dinner with my creepy stalker.

"Earth to Cate." Sonia's voice cut into my thoughts. "Are you planning to make that coffee or not?"

I glanced behind and saw three people waiting to use the machine, and heat rose up my cheeks. "Uh, yes."

Espresso in hand, I headed off for another day in the fun factory.

***

The next week, Marie really did bring popcorn. She was munching on a handful when I walked in, and as I sat down, she offered the bag to me.

"Want some?"

"Thanks." I'd skipped lunch so I wouldn't be late for class. All I'd had today was a smoothie after my half-hearted attempt at yoga in the spare room. "Ugh! What flavour is this?"

She shrugged and looked at the bag. "Watermelon. They were giving it away for free outside the Tube station."

There was a good reason for that. Who would ever pay for something so disgusting? "It's horrid."

"Yeah, I've tasted better. But, you know, free."

I'd want paid to eat it. "So, what's the plan today?"

"Same as last week for me."

"Ogling and sketching the naughty bits?"

"Yup. How about you?"

"I thought I'd try acrylics."

My stomach growled as I set up a canvas on one of the easels Delores kept in the store cupboard, but all thoughts of food disappeared when Joe climbed onto the dais. Well, they didn't vanish completely—I developed a sudden craving for sausage and meatballs as he dropped the sheet and perched on the stool.

Full frontal. Full freaking frontal. And believe me, his property was definitely worth starting a dispute over. He kept his eyes firmly fixed on the wall beyond, which was a good thing because if he'd looked straight at me, he'd have sucked me in like a tractor beam and I might have been tempted to crawl over and lick something I shouldn't.

"Fuck me," Marie whispered. "Is he part donkey?"

No, horse. I didn't dare to reply because if my tongue rolled out of my mouth, I'd never get it back in again.

Up front, Delores grinned like the Cheshire Cat and clapped her hands. Some of the glitter she'd decorated her hair with dropped off and floated onto Joe's bits, twinkling away like magic fairy dust. I couldn't take my eyes off it. Him. His bits. Wow.

"Ladies, I know having a live model can be a little, er, distracting." Half the class sniggered while the glazed expressions on the others matched my own. "But we only have two hours. So I suggest you start drawing if you want to immortalise this view on paper to take home with you."

With some effort, I picked up a pencil to sketch Joe's outline and dragged my attention to his face. Week one, he'd shown a hint of a smile, but today his expression was a mix of concentration and mild discomfort. Was it the stool? Perhaps Delores should have offered him a cushion? Hell, I'd have fetched him one myself if it made him look happier.

For the next two hours, I blocked out everything and lost myself in painting the man sitting before me. Occasionally he'd shift an inch, or twitch his nose like he had an itch, a reminder that sitting around while a bunch of horny women rendered him on canvas wasn't the nicest job in the world. Quite apart from the fact that he had to do it stark bollock naked. Did he pose for students a lot? For some reason, the idea of him stripping off in front of other groups made me clench my jaw.

Was that...jealousy?

Cate, you're being completely irrational. This was the man's job. I forced those feelings away, and they were quickly replaced by a new thought: if he did model for other groups, which ones, and how fast could I sign up?

"Can I borrow your sharpener?" Marie whispered towards the end.

Concentration broken, I handed it over and took the opportunity to look at her drawing. When she stopped salivating, Marie really was a talented artist, and her picture blew me away. She'd captured Joe's expression perfectly and, predictably, his naughty bits.

"What do you think?" she asked.

"Gorgeous."

"And the drawing?"

I scrunched my lips to the side. "Okay, I guess."

She giggled as she leaned over to look at my canvas. "You like the abs, huh?"

Oh dear, was it that obvious? "At least I painted his face too."

"Barely. Hey, I've got a new idea for a class—blindfolded painting. We have to feel our way around the subjects."

"But if we're wearing blindfolds, how will we see to paint?"

"Don't get so hung up on the details, Cate."

But my whole life, I'd been paid to get hung up on the details. So many times I'd wished I could be more like Marie—relaxed, outgoing, maybe a little impulsive. But as I snuck a couple of glances at Joe while we packed our things away, I couldn't even bring myself to say hello to him.

"Hey," Miguel said, leaning over. "Did you hear what happened with Mandy?"

I'd noticed the empty seat. The girl I'd caught photographing Joe in the first week hadn't turned up today. "The pretty blonde girl?"

He nodded.

"No, what happened?"

"Apparently, she hung around last week and asked Joe if he'd like to come back to her place."

My legs began shaking. "And?"

"He knocked her back, even when she lifted her top up to show him what he'd be missing."

Wow. She offered it to him on a plate and he said no? Oh, who was I kidding? Joe surely had a girlfriend, and I had to admire him for staying faithful. The perfect man. The perfect fantasy.

And I still had two weeks left to admire him.

CHAPTER 5

I DITHERED AROUND packing up until Delores gave Joe his sheet back. Before she handed it over, she hesitated for a few seconds, just out of reach, and her gaze dropped down to his package. Ever the professional, he kept his eyes fixed elsewhere rather than blushing like any normal person. Once he'd wrapped the sheet around his waist and disappeared, I stored my still-damp painting in the rack to dry until next week, then stowed my paints and brushes.

Two weeks left.

Marie gave me a quick hug before she dashed off to catch the Tube. "Andy promised me the goods if I got home quickly, and after that session, I need whatever he's offering."

"Too much information."

She took a step back, holding me at arm's length, and shook her head. "Really? No. Too much information would be if I described the way his—"

"Stop!" I put my hand over her mouth and hugged her again. "Just go already."

Left alone, I may—may—have hung around in case Joe reappeared, not to speak to him, but just to get a final glimpse. You know, of him with clothes on. Something to feed my dreams through the next six days. But he didn't come back, and eventually I gave up.

I was a little dazed as I wandered out into the street, and when something lumpy and black bounced off the front of a passing van and landed at my feet with a soft *thud*, I did the only sensible thing and squealed.

"Eeeeeeaaaaahhhhh!"

What the hell was it? I'd dropped my bag, and pencils rolled across the pavement into the gutter, but that didn't matter anymore when the lump moved. I dropped to a crouch beside it. A cat. Oh, my goodness, a tiny black cat, and judging by the awkward angle of its leg and the blood spreading out beneath it, a badly injured cat.

"Shh, shh, tiny one. I'll get you to a vet, don't worry."

But how? A quick glance showed an empty street, devoid of any passers-by or, more importantly, cabs. The cat let out a pathetic *miaow*, and a tear rolled down my cheek and plopped to the flagstones.

"What happened?" A soft voice behind made me jump out of my skin, and I turned around to find a blurry figure leaning over.

"Hit and run. The poor thing's hurt really badly."

The man knelt beside me and tore off his jacket before gently scooping the kitty into it. The way it whimpered made my tears fall even harder.

"Can you wait here with it while I run to the main road and flag down a cab?" he asked.

I managed to nod as he passed the bundle over, not that my legs would have carried me anywhere. At least the cat was still breathing; that was something at least. What could I do? How could I make it more comfortable?

The sound of an engine made me look up, and a car door slammed. Then Joe was taking the cat out of my arms and shoving the remains of my art stuff into my bag. Joe? As I wiped my eyes with my sleeve, I realised that's who my saviour was. And not only that, the cab driver was female, middle-aged, and staring at his butt. No wonder she'd stopped so quickly.

A few pencils had been run over by the wheels, but who cared? Pencils could be replaced, but the cat's life couldn't. Joe put my bag in the back and held out a hand for me.

"Are you coming?"

"Uh...yes."

I barely had time to register that he was touching me before I was sitting beside him, close, very close, and he looked down at the cat.

"Do you know if there's a vet near here? Or shall I google?"

"Yes, it's not far. I take my own cats there, and they've always got a vet on call for emergencies."

That was why I registered at that particular place. After chasing around London in the early hours when Thor managed to choke on a salmon bone one night three years ago, I'd switched practices because it wasn't an experience I cared to repeat. Voice shaking, I garbled the address for the driver, she smiled at Joe, and we took off.

Joe clutched at my waist as the cab cornered on two wheels, then made a grab for the cat before it slid off the seat.

"Seat belt," he whispered, struggling one-handed with his own.

"Got it."

Between us, we wedged our feet and arms so neither we nor our precious cargo came to any more harm on the wild ride through London's darkened streets. I even managed to gather my wits enough to call Mr. Fraser, the kindly vet who looked after Thor and Loki, before we arrived. He was standing in the doorway as we pulled up in a puff of tyre smoke, and Joe pushed a twenty-pound note at our wannabe Lewis Hamilton before we tumbled out of the cab. If ever business got slow, she could make a pretty penny racing the Grand Prix.

In the waiting room, Mr. Fraser peered at his patient as a pretty nurse appeared behind him. She didn't pay much attention to the cat, far more interested in checking Joe out instead. Not that I could blame her. He'd put on a pair of well-worn jeans and a snug black T-shirt, but I knew what he was hiding underneath them, and despite the dire situation, my nipples stood to attention. A quick glance down at my shirt revealed the extent of my problem, and I hurriedly tugged my jacket closed.

"This little girl's got a broken femur by the looks of things," Mr. Fraser said. "And we'll need to close up this nasty hole in her side. Whose cat is she?" He looked from me to Joe.

"Neither of ours," he said.

"I was just leaving my art class when a van drove into her right in front of me." I closed my eyes and willed away the lump that rose in my throat as my mind replayed the sickening *crunch*. "The guy drove off. Didn't even stop. But I'll pay for whatever needs to be done if you can save her, the poor thing."

As if on cue, the cat raised her head half an inch

and let out a whimper.

"I'm sure we can do something," Mr. Fraser said. "Do you want to wait while I do an initial examination?"

"Yes, please." When I looked at Joe, he was nodding too.

Once I'd sat on one of the orange plastic chairs, the adrenaline buzz from our dash across town began to wear off. I clutched my hands in my lap to stop them from shaking. Joe settled in the seat beside me, and my heart began beating in a wild staccato. It was so loud in my ears that I worried he might hear it too. But when I risked a glance to the side, he was staring straight ahead at a poster advising on the importance of regular worming.

He may have looked relaxed in the void that stretched between us, but eventually my nerves could take it no longer.

"Thanks for coming with me."

"What sort of man would I be if I left a lady to deal with that alone?"

"Still, thanks."

Silence descended again as I learned all about the life cycle of fleas from the wall frieze opposite. Boy, they were ugly little suckers. The list of pet boarding services on the notice board became equally fascinating, not that I ever needed to use them because I never went on holiday. When I was dating the accountant, I'd googled beach destinations in my lunch breaks and even gone so far as to make myself a top ten of luxury resorts I wanted to visit, but then he'd mentioned his allergy to sand and that was that. If only I were braver, I could have gone on a singles cruise or booked one of those fancy tour packages, but face it, there was a better chance of Simon Cowell becoming prime minister than that happening.

Joe cleared his throat, and I jumped out of my skin.

"You like cats, then?" he asked.

"I've got two of my own." I could feel his gaze on me. "How about you?"

"Had an old tabby when I was a kid."

"And now?"

"Wouldn't work with my living situation."

"Difficult landlord?"

"Something like that."

"I've had plenty of those over the years. Can you believe the last one asked if I'd had Thor and Loki declawed? And when I told him I hadn't, he insisted on triple the deposit and refused to return it when I left, even though there wasn't any damage and I'd repainted every room. I had to write several strongly worded letters to get my money back, so it's lucky I'm a lawyer, although I really hate getting into arguments and..."

Dammit, what on earth was I talking about? Joe's mere presence had made me ramble on like a madwoman. I looked down at the green-and-white linoleum, wishing it would swallow me up, but no hole appeared, and Joe's quiet chuckle made me want to barge through the double doors at the back of the room and put myself to sleep.

"Thor and Loki?" he asked. "You're into the Marvel movies?"

"Uh, no, I've long held a deep fascination for Norse mythology."

"I've always been a comic book guy, but I did read the Poetic Edda a few years back."

"The what?"

His chuckle became a full-blown laugh. "I knew it. So, Hemsworth or Hiddleston?"

Dammit, what the hell was an Edda? "Uh, Hemsworth," I blurted before my mouth caught up with my brain. The blond. The blond who bore a disturbing similarity to Joe.

A smile played across his lips as my nervousness threatened to turn into a freak-out. What was it my father used to say? If you're scared of speaking to somebody, just imagine them naked. Well, I didn't have to imagine, and thinking of Joe's generously sized bits didn't help matters. My eyes dropped to his crotch before I could stop them, and when I dragged them up again, I found he'd watched me do it. Aw, hell.

"Would it help if I stripped off again?"

My eyes bugged out as he continued.

"I mean, would it help you be less nervous?"

I took a deep breath and forced myself to enunciate each word carefully. "No, I don't think that would help."

Well, I got the words out, but I sounded like a prissy snob when I did it. This was a disaster. An absolute disaster. Joe was the hottest man I'd ever attempted to have a conversation with, and so far I'd uttered every word with my foot firmly in my mouth.

Wow, this floor was really interesting.

"Kate? Is your name Kate?"

"Cate with a C. How did you know?"

"I heard the girl you sit next to call you that." Out of the corner of my eye, I saw him give a little shudder. "She makes me nervous."

"What? Why?"

"Because she eyes me up like I'm lunch."

A bubble of laughter escaped. "You don't need to worry. She's got a boyfriend."

"Thank goodness. The one last week didn't, and I didn't know how to get away."

"I heard she flashed her...er..."

"Yeah. She wasn't shy. Even when Delores asked her to leave, she still tried to give me her phone number. This art modelling's harder than I thought."

"You haven't done it before?"

He shook his head. "Never. Only did it this time because one of the guys at the gym needed a favour. His new girlfriend wasn't too keen on the idea of him stripping off for a bunch of ladies and put her foot down."

"What about your girlfriend?"

Oh, hell, did I really ask that? It made me sound jealous, didn't it? And needy. And nosy.

"That's not an issue."

What did that mean? That he didn't have a girlfriend? Or he had one and she didn't mind? Or... or... Was he gay?

I didn't know what to say, so I resorted to reading the notice board again. Home-made kitty treats for sale? Hmm, Thor and Loki might like some of those.

Mr. Fraser saved us from another awkward silence by pushing through the door as he peeled off a pair of latex gloves. I tried to read the expression on his face, but his frown didn't give much away.

"Well, I've stitched up the cut, but if we want to repair that break, it's not going to be cheap. And without an owner..."

"What are the other options?" I asked.

"She's comfortable on painkillers for now, and a cheaper option would be to remove the leg. I can call some of the local cat charities in the morning to see if any of them would be willing to help."

"And what if they won't?"

"I wish I could save every cat for free, but finances won't allow it, I'm afraid."

My heart lurched. He wanted to put the cat down? No way, not if an operation might help. "I'll pay. Please, try to save her leg."

"It could run to a couple of thousand, and if you can't track down the owner..." He shook his head. "From the state of her, she might not even have one. She's far too thin."

"It doesn't matter, I'll pay," I repeated. My conscience wouldn't let an animal suffer, and what else would I do with my money? Spend it on my buzzing social life?

Mr. Fraser put a hand on my shoulder and gave me a tired smile. "We'll stabilise her tonight, and if she's strong enough in the morning, we'll operate. I'll do my best to keep the costs down. You're a good person, Cate."

I stifled a yawn. "And a tired person."

"Time for your young man to get you home."

"Oh, he's not my—"

Joe's hand on the small of my back startled me. "I'll get her home."

CHAPTER 6

"IT'S OKAY, HONESTLY. I can get home by myself," I said to Joe, my back burning from the touch of his hand as we walked along the dark high street. Fraser's Veterinary Surgery took up a double storefront between a hair salon and a florist, and Mr. Fraser told me when I first went there that he lived in the flat above so he could be on hand for the animals. Now, the shops were silent, with music from the pub on the corner providing the backdrop to our conversation as revellers spilled out onto the pavement.

"It's almost midnight, and Thursday night is drinking night," Joe said. "My mother brought me up to make sure a lady got home safely at the end of the night."

I echoed Mr. Fraser's words to me. "She's a good woman."

Joe nodded but didn't smile. "She was."

Was? He'd lost his mother? I never knew what to say in these situations, whether to gush sympathy or change the subject. A simple "I'm sorry" seemed inadequate. Fortunately, or unfortunately depending on how you looked at it, fate intervened with a loose paving slab for me to trip over, and before I could catch my balance, I landed in the gutter as a car whizzed past inches from my outstretched foot.

"Fuck!" Joe grabbed me under my armpits and hauled me backwards into a shop doorway. "Are you okay? Did the car touch you?"

"No, I'm fine." I tried to put a brave face on things as I stood there in one shoe, plastered against a man I only ever looked stupid in front of. Another vehicle sped past and my near miss sunk in, how the black tyres had been so close I felt the whoosh of air. "Honestly, I'm good."

"You're shaking."

"That's probably just because I didn't have lunch."

"Hold on."

Joe propped me against the wall while he retrieved my kitten heel from the kerbside, then crouched to slide my foot into it.

Please, say my feet aren't too sweaty. This evening was turning into a disaster of epic proportions.

"Why didn't you have lunch, Cate?"

"A meeting overran, then I had a report to write and a client called. If I'd stopped to eat, I wouldn't have made it to art class." And I'd have missed the chance to embarrass myself completely in front of a man who kept a python in his pants. A true tragedy.

"We need to fix that. Can you walk? Or do you want me to find a cab?"

"I can walk." Well, hobble. "My apartment isn't far."

Joe wrapped an arm around my waist, and suddenly the whole near-death experience didn't seem so bad. The warmth of his arm seeped through my jacket, jumper, and blouse, leaving my skin aflame as his fingers brushed me softly with each step. For a moment, I considered stumbling again. If I twisted an ankle, would he carry me?

With his touch so distracting, I didn't notice where we were going until he pushed open a door and steered me into a brightly lit café. Not a posh place, more of a greasy spoon with a veritable smorgasbord of fried food listed on a chipped blackboard behind the counter.

"What are we doing here?"

"I'm not taking you home until you've eaten something."

"Really, you don't have to do that. I'm not even all that hungry."

Damn my traitorous stomach. It let out a grumble akin to a nearby earthquake, telling everyone for miles around that I secretly craved a plate of chips. With vinegar and ketchup, and maybe a cheeseburger to go with them.

"What can I get you, love?" the lady behind the counter asked Joe.

I clutched at his arm to stop him from going closer. "I'm supposed to be on a diet," I whispered.

"I don't usually eat this kind of food either, so let's call it a cheat day, shall we?"

Oh, hell. If he kept smiling at me like that, I'd quite happily chow down on a plate of deep-fried locusts with a side order of worms. "Maybe just a small portion."

"Two of the all-day breakfasts and a couple of teas, please," Joe requested and handed over a twenty-pound note.

How strange had this evening ended up? From good to awful and now surreal as I prepared to munch my way through a grease mountain with the man who'd invaded my thoughts for every moment of the last three weeks. *Every* moment. I'd accidentally written his name instead of my client's on a deposition yesterday, and Reggie, my intern, knew something was up when he informed me Joe was on the phone and I dropped my coffee.

"How did he get my number?" I'd wondered out loud as the stain spread across my desk.

Reggie gave me that look of surprise mixed with indifference that only a nineteen-year-old could manage and handed me a wad of paper towels. "Who? Joe, the mailroom clerk? I expect he looked it up in the internal directory like anybody else."

Of course. *That* Joe. Sixty-something Joe, who'd collected my post every day since I started working at Berkeley, Rogers and Smyth. I shrugged and laughed off my stupidity, but for the rest of the day, Reggie had given me odd looks, a bit like sexy Joe was doing now.

"Are you okay? You seem distracted."

"Just thinking about the, uh, cat."

"It's a fighter. Did you see it gripping my hand with its claws in the taxi?"

I shook my head, noticing the blood spots on Joe's knuckles for the first time. "Are you okay? Do you need to get a tetanus shot?"

"All up to date. The army doctors were sticklers for that kind of thing."

"You were in the army?"

"Until last year."

Sweat gathered on the back of my neck as visions of Joe dressed in camouflage swam through my mind. Think Jeremy Renner in *The Hurt Locker*, except without a shirt, obviously. Maybe a set of those dog tags around his neck. Or...or...or what about in a dress uniform, like *Tom Cruise in A Few Good Men?* Can you tell I had a Netflix subscription and a tragic lack of a life outside my apartment? Hmm, I might even pick GI Joe over Joe the naked art model.

"Are you sure you're okay?"

Oh, good grief, I couldn't think straight around this man. Thankfully, the lady plonked two paper cups of tea down on the counter and yelled that they were ready. Joe gave me a brief concerned look before he got up to fetch them. *Cate, get a bloody grip.*

"I put a couple of sugars in yours," Joe said as he sat down again. "You look like you need them."

Was that a polite way of telling me I looked worse for wear? Probably, and I couldn't exactly argue with that assessment. "Thank you."

He'd added plenty of milk too, and I took a sip, sneaking another glance at him over the rim of the cup. This outing felt a little awkward. What on earth was I supposed to say to him? Most of my previous dates had been happy enough to talk about themselves, but Joe didn't seem so chatty. Should I attempt to start the conversation? What should I say? I knew so little about him, only that he'd once been in the army and he looked really, really good without his clothes on.

I spent a minute lining up the salt and pepper shakers and ketchup, resisting the urge to wipe away a dribble of sauce running down the outside of the bottle. And he just kept watching me.

"Uh, do you go to the gym often?" I blurted.

Well done, Cate. Congratulations. Move the topic to a subject you clearly know nothing about.

"I work there."

Ah, yes, that did explain a lot. And it also meant Joe spent his days surrounded by toned lovelies who didn't have to worry about muffin top, except on the organic apple-and-wheat-germ versions they undoubtedly nibbled on for brunch while sipping their decaff.

"I should get a membership." Dammit. Why did I say that? Now I sounded like a stalker. "Not necessarily your gym," I hastened to add. "But *a* gym."

"Hmmm."

What did "hmmm" mean? Yes, I definitely needed to lose a stone or two? No, I was a lost cause? What?

I didn't get the chance to ask before the lady brought our food over. Oh, wonderful. A sausage. Two fried tomatoes. Was there anything that didn't remind me of Joe's naughty bits? I picked up my cutlery, unsure where to start. The fried egg. The egg was safe.

Joe didn't seem to share my reservations as he chopped his sausage into bits and forked one into his mouth. That sexy mouth with full pink lips. Good grief, what was wrong with me? I hadn't even been drinking.

I gingerly took a mouthful of food, praying the kitchen met the relevant hygiene standards. I'd never eaten in an establishment like this, ever, not even when I was a student. The college had provided all my meals, and since I went to Oxford, that ranged from a healthy salad up to a three-course dinner with wine and roast pheasant. Giving in to my father's wishes with regards to my career choice had provided me with a few perks, at least.

But none of them included men who were sexy as sin with a kind heart to boot. Joe was a real catch. And even though I could stretch an arm out and touch him, he was way out of my reach.

My phone pinged with a message, interrupting my thoughts, and I made the mistake of picking it up.

Marie: Flipping heck. Still fanning myself after

tonight's session. Joe is hereby known as Mr. Hot Rod.

Worse, she'd accompanied the message with a hand-drawn dick pic, done in charcoal on cream paper. The piece of egg slid down the wrong way, and I coughed and spluttered as I tried to get my breath back.

"Can we get a glass of water?" Joe called out to the lady, and one appeared almost instantly. "Here, drink this."

He crouched beside me and rubbed my back until the gagging subsided, although if I'd choked, that would have saved me from dying of embarrassment when I followed his gaze to my phone.

"Is that...?"

"Uh, I think so. Maybe. It's Marie's idea of a joke."

"Mr. Hot Rod?"

I watched in horror as another line of text popped up on the screen: *Just a not-so-little something to give you sweet dreams tonight.*

My cheeks turned the same colour as the fried tomatoes as Joe walked back to his seat, chuckling, and I had no idea what to say. Should I offer to erase the picture? I snuck another glance at it. Hmm, it was actually quite good. *Dammit, Cate.* I could hardly tell Marie I was busy eating dinner with the object of her perverted affections, so I turned my phone off and shoved it into my handbag, half hoping the flipping thing broke.

A smirk played across Joe's lips as he finished his meal, but I couldn't meet his eyes. And the food held even less appeal now, but I made the effort to eat most of it because Joe had bought it.

"Do you want anything else?" he asked as he popped his last piece of fried bread into his mouth.

I quickly shook my head, vowing to drag myself out of bed tomorrow morning to put on one of the aerobics DVDs. Without anybody watching my gawky attempts at coordination, I'd found the exercise wasn't quite as horrible as usual.

"Time to go?" he asked.

"Yes."

"How does your ankle feel?"

I stood up, testing it out. "Not so bad. I think it was more shock than anything else that affected me earlier."

Outside, the clear sky left a chill in the air, and I shivered as the door to the café closed behind us. The crowds from the pub on the corner had disappeared, and the lack of music meant the thumping of my heart was all too obvious.

"Which way?" Joe asked.

"Left."

"Are you cold?"

"A little, but I'll be home soon."

"I'd offer you my jacket, but the cat already had that." He paused, then held an arm out. "Here."

The shudder that ran through me as Joe settled his arm over my shoulders had nothing to do with the cold and everything to do with his touch. I resisted the urge to lean into him as I wondered what to do with my spare arm. I longed to wrap it around his waist and slip my hand into the back pocket of his jeans, but in the end I opted to hold it awkwardly in front of me. After all, this arrangement was purely for warmth. Nothing more.

The walk back to my apartment only took five minutes, and for once I wished I lived on the other side of London. Maybe even in the Home Counties or Scotland, because I could have snuggled against Joe forever, thinking dirty thoughts that made Marie's message look tame in comparison.

But all too soon, we were outside Heron Court.

"You did a good thing saving that cat tonight," Joe said. "Most people would have walked right by."

"I hate to see animals hurt, and it's me who should be thanking you. I'd have struggled to look after the cat and find a taxi on my own." And not freak out and burst into tears.

Joe shifted uncomfortably. "I wish I could pay some of the costs, but I'm a bit short right now."

That must have taken a lot for him to say. Most men would have kept quiet rather than dent their pride with an admission like that. "Honestly, it's okay. I don't have much else to spend my money on at the moment." I dug around in my handbag. "And here, let me give you something towards the cab and food."

He took a step backwards, then another. "No. That was on me."

"But—"

"I'm not taking money off you, Cate."

Maybe I shouldn't have made the offer. I'd embarrassed him, hadn't I? Dammit, why was I so bad at this talking-to-guys thing? I needed to think of something smart to salvage the situation, but in the end, all that came out was a quiet, "Thank you."

"I'll see you next week?" he asked.

"Yes, I'll be there." Not even Mr. Berkeley and his ever-expanding to-do list could keep me away.

As Joe disappeared into the darkness, I glanced up to my apartment on the top floor, then tracked right to the lit window next door. Was it me, or did Dane's curtain just move?

CHAPTER 7

MY ALARM CLOCK went off at 6 a.m., and all my good intentions of doing aerobics before work came out in one long, drawn-out groan. Maybe I could just turn over and sleep for another half hour? But then the events of last night came flooding back, including the mountain of fried food I'd munched through and the complete mortification I'd suffered at the hands of Marie, and I dragged myself out of bed because otherwise I'd just have lain there and stressed about it.

At least I only had to go as far as the third bedroom, and at least I could wear a sports bra which, being honest, didn't smell that fresh, teamed up with a pair of leggings with holes in the thighs that I really should have thrown away months ago.

The endorphins from my workout, or perhaps the sheer relief at having burnt off the calorific equivalent of a fried egg and sausage, meant I sidestepped Dane's latest offering of a frappuccino and a set of hot-pink sweatbands with a smile on my face, and as I poured yet another cup of Starbucks' finest down the sink, I mentally added another item to today's to-do list, which was growing longer by the second: find a photo of Dane.

Bloody men. If the world were full of lesbians, life would be so much simpler. Except then Marie would be sending me tit pics, probably.

When I got to work, Reggie was already at his desk outside my office, typing away.

"Berkeley stopped by. He wants to catch up on the Dartington case."

"Dartington's lawyer's stalling. Nothing's changed since our last discussion."

"Two whole days ago, I know. I did try to tell him that, but hey, I'm just the intern."

Reggie may have been young, and Berkeley may only have hired him because he needed a black person so he'd look as if he were paying more than lip service to the company's diversity and inclusion policy, but he was smarter than my last two assistants put together.

"I get it, and he only listens to me when he feels like it. Maybe when we're both fifty..."

Reggie rolled his eyes and pointed at the cup of coffee on the end of his desk. "I got your espresso. What's the plan for today, boss?"

"I have a meeting with a new client at nine, some research to do on Antisocial Behaviour Orders relating to the height of trees, and in the afternoon, I need to draft the sales contract for that shopping mall in Nottingham."

"And Berkeley?"

"I'll stop by his office, but I need to make a call first."

The poor kitty had preyed on my mind all the way around the Circle Line, and the vet's would be open now. Had she survived the night?

A harried-sounding receptionist answered the phone, but once I gave my name her tone warmed up.

"Ah, yes, Miss Jenkins. The little black cat. Mr.

Fraser's pinning her leg right at this moment, and we're all rooting for her."

"Could you call me when the operation's finished?"

"Of course."

Two more hours, three cups of coffee, and two meetings passed before Mr. Fraser himself rang with good news, and I let myself smile at last.

"Your little cat's a fighter. Just coming round from the anaesthetic, so she's groggy, but the operation went as well as we could have hoped."

"Thank goodness."

"Which brings us to our second problem. She'll need to keep the cast on for six weeks while the bone heals properly, and she'll need somewhere quiet to recuperate. Do you want us to start looking for a charity to take her?"

I'd already thought about that during my sleepless night. "I'm going to put up posters looking for her owners, but if nobody comes forward, she can stay with me. As long as she gets on okay with Thor and Loki, I'll keep her."

Okay, so three felines would put me in crazy cat woman territory, but with the number of stupid things I'd done lately, that seemed somehow fitting. And in the short time I'd known her, that little kitty had left a big impression, not to mention being indirectly responsible for my non-date with the sexiest man I'd ever met. Probably I owed her for that one.

"I had a feeling you'd say that. Feel free to visit in the meantime."

I was shopping on eBay for cat accessories when Reggie walked in with a pile of ASBO research, all neatly stapled and alphabetised. I tried to minimise the window, but instead I ended up with a screen full of Facebook, where I may have had a photo of Dane on view, wearing that creepy grin of his as he posed for a selfie.

Reggie raised an eyebrow. "Is that why you've been so distracted lately?"

"What, Dane? No! Well, sort of, I guess."

"Is he the guy who goes with that?"

Reggie pointed at the corner of my legal pad, where I'd accidentally doodled Joe's buttocks during my last conference call, and I clapped one hand over my mouth while I used the other to screw the paper up and launch it at the bin. Of course I missed, and Reggie corrected my mistake with a wide grin on his face.

Then he reached out to my printer and plucked the picture of Dane from the tray. "Isn't this a bit big for carrying around in your wallet? I can show you how to reduce the size if you want."

"No need. That's not for my wallet; it's for my dartboard." Wonderful, now I sounded even more insane. Three cats, remember? It was all because of the cats. "It's therapeutic, okay?"

"Ooooooookaaaaaaay. You want me to print out a photo of Berkeley for you? And Sonia? She was bitching at the water cooler again this morning."

"Uh, I already have those pinned up."

Reggie laughed. "I knew there was a reason I liked you."

At least someone did. "What's Sonia been moaning about this time? Me?"

"Nah, not today. You know that tall dude who works for the investment firm next door?"

We all did, even Reggie it seemed. I may have

secretly snapped a candid shot of him while we queued for lunch in the deli along the road, and it might have somehow found its way onto Marie's phone. And that could possibly be how he'd earned the nickname of "Joystick."

"Yes, I've seen him around."

"You want me to print a picture of him too?"

"No!" I cleared my throat. "What did Sonia have to say?"

"She heard he was big on charity work, so she volunteered to help out at the same place because she wants to get in his pants, and now she has to, and I quote, 'spend my evenings serving slop to the bunch of vagrants who clutter up the pavements during the day.'"

"Wow. What a nasty thing to say."

"I almost threw your coffee over her. We didn't all grow up in posh mansions with Daddy's money to spend."

And Sonia's comment had clearly touched a nerve with Reggie. He didn't speak about his background much, but I knew he'd grown up on a council estate in a bad part of town. The lady from Human Resources mentioned it when she was crowing about how this made Berkeley, Rogers and Smyth such a "wonderfully diverse" place to work. I'd always imagined she had the equivalent of an HR bingo card stapled to her office wall—she'd managed to check off "gay" two months ago, when she proudly announced Matthew's sexuality before he turned up for his first day, and rumour had it she was looking for a receptionist who used a wheelchair, preferably from an ethnic minority.

But I'd lucked out and got Reggie, who was more

fun than my last three interns put together, and he typed better too, seeing as he didn't have inch-long acrylic nails to get in the way.

And even though I *had* grown up in a posh house with a generous father, I identified more with Reggie than Sonia, whose rich daddy most probably had a pointy tail and horns.

"It's tempting to throw something at her, isn't it? But don't do anything that could get you fired. Who else would do my incredibly exciting analysis of the footfall in West Quay Shopping Centre?"

"Is that this afternoon's task?"

"Sorry. But, uh, I was hoping you'd be able to do me a favour first."

"What kind of favour?"

"Could you make me some posters? I found this cat last night, and I need to try and track down her owner."

"What sort of cat? Like, a kitten?"

"A little older. She got hit by a car and I took her to the vet." Best to leave Joe out of this, because I didn't have time for the inevitable questions.

"Is that why you look so tired?"

Great, thanks, Reggie. Way to make a girl feel pretty. "I didn't get home until late."

"Sure, I'll make the posters. I used to feed this stray cat that lived behind our block of flats when I was a kid. You got a photo I can use?"

"No, but I'll ask the receptionist at the vet's to send one over."

***

By the end of the afternoon, I had a stack of full-colour,

laminated posters courtesy of Reggie, a dry throat from the four phone calls I'd just made, one after the other, and a headache. I was just rummaging through my desk drawer in search of an elusive packet of paracetamol when my mobile rang.

Marie. She usually texted, so what was so important? My heart lurched at the first thought that came into my head.

"Hello? Tell me Delores hasn't cancelled next week's class."

"She hasn't. Why would you think that?"

"Uh..." Sheer panic at the thought of not seeing Joe again? Purely so I could update him on the cat, you understand. "I don't know. Why are you calling?"

"Because if I just texted, you'd come up with an excuse not to go, and that's not happening."

"Excuse not to go where?"

"One of my suppliers has given me two tickets to the 'Underwear Through the Ages' exhibition at the V&A, and I need someone to go with."

"What about Andy?"

"Andy claimed he's washing his hair any day I want to go."

"Underwear? Seriously?"

"What, has Delores been spoiling you? You've got used to seeing Mr. Hot Rod without his tighty-whities and you can't bear to look at a pair of boxers ever again?"

"You can't keep calling him that. What if he finds out?"

Or rather, what if he already had?

"Hmm, you're right. It makes him sound like a boy racer, and he's all man. What about Torpedo?"

"No! Besides, he was in the army, not the navy."

Silence. Oops.

Then Marie's voice, tinged with curiosity. "And how do you know that?"

"Uh, I think Delores might have mentioned it."

"Don't give me that, lady. I'm positive I'd have remembered a juicy little snippet like that. Where did you really hear it?"

"I might have talked to him after class. But don't get too excited," I added hastily.

My words fell on deaf ears. Mine, by the time Marie finished squealing. I held the phone away as my head throbbed. Where was that blasted packet of paracetamol?

"What did you talk about? How long for? Does he sound as hot as he looks?"

Marie may have been the closest friend I had, but when it came to my love life, or rather the lack of it, her meddling knew no bounds. I still cringed every time I recalled the blind date she'd set me up on with an old school friend of hers after the accountant dumped me. He'd taken me out to a Mexican place, and despite the fact it was early evening, he'd yawned all the way through the starter. During one particularly wide effort, he'd stretched his arms out and accidentally knocked over a vase of flowers. The vase hit a menu, which landed on a candle, which tipped onto the tablecloth and set it on fire. Luckily, a quick-thinking waiter threw a carafe of water over the flames, but half of it landed on me and my white top went see-through. We'd left pretty quickly after that.

Now, I could have written one awful date off as an accident, but desperate to make amends, Marie had set me up with a colleague the following week. He took me to his parents' Italian restaurant, because, he confessed, it meant our dinner would be free, and he got his mother to call me the next day to ask how I thought our date went. When I broke the news there wouldn't be a second, he'd texted me to say he didn't date fat bitches, anyway. Now, I didn't stand a chance with Joe, but I really didn't need Marie's help in screwing things up.

No, I was capable of that all by myself. After the Italian debacle, I'd joined Tinder in a fit of margarita-induced desperation. After accidentally swiping right instead of left, I felt too guilty to back out when the guy announced he'd bought a new suit especially for our date. Except when he said "suit," he meant "tracksuit," and we'd spent a painful hour in Burger King. When I came back from using the toilet, I'd caught him browsing the very app we'd met on in search of a girl not so, in his words, "snooty posh."

It was at that point I'd decided to focus on my career for a bit.

So, while Marie only ever meant well, telling her about the cat, the cab ride, and my non-date with Joe would have been an invitation for disaster.

"We didn't talk about much at all. He just mentioned his past job in passing as we walked outside."

"He didn't hang around to chat?" Disappointment tinged her voice.

"No, he seemed like he was in a hurry."

"Ah well, there's always next week. And if he's ex-army, I've got a new nickname for him—Chief of Staff."

"Do you ever stop?"

"Nope, and you love it really. So tell me, are you coming to the V&A? The tickets are valid until the end of the year."

"Okay, I'll come."

"I'll be keeping my fingers crossed for that too."

CHAPTER 8

I SPENT AN hour that evening taping Reggie's posters to bus stops, phone booths, and lamp posts, and by the time I got home, I was exhausted from the walking and a long day at work. My fingers itched to dial for a pizza, but I resisted the urge and rummaged through the fridge until I remembered I hadn't ordered any groceries this week. Thank goodness Yo Sushi delivered.

And quickly too. The entry phone buzzed half an hour later and the grinning delivery guy waved at the camera. A minute later, knuckles rapped on my door, and I opened it to find...

"Dane? What do you want?"

He held up my bag of sushi. "The delivery driver was in a hurry, so I offered to help him out. Looks like you've ordered enough for two. Expecting a guest?" He stood on tiptoes and peered past me.

"No, I'm not. Give that here."

"Maybe I could join you, then?"

And maybe you could take a hike off the roof. "Sorry, but I was looking forward to a quiet evening."

"How about I take you out for dinner next week instead?"

"I'm busy."

"The week after?"

"Work's very demanding at the moment."

"Come on, Cate. You need to take a few hours off every now and then."

I managed a grimace before I snatched the bag off him and backed into my flat. "I like my job, thank you very much."

By the time I slammed the door, I was breathing hard. Did Dane have nothing better to do all day than interfere in my life? Couldn't he see how creepy his behaviour was? And how dare he make that comment about my menu choices? Most of the food was salad, for crying out loud, and now I'd lost my appetite completely. A tear popped out as I shoved the whole bag into the fridge and retreated to the sofa with a glass of fruit juice. Okay, Chardonnay. It was Chardonnay. Why couldn't I have a nice little old lady living next door, one who smiled politely in the hallway, played bingo in the evenings, and didn't watch my every move then judge my lifestyle?

***

Four days passed in a blur of work, Netflix, Waitrose ready meals, daydreams about Joe, and emailed pictures of hot men in uniform from Marie before I got the call I'd been waiting for. Kitty could come home.

Up until then, I'd avoided tempting fate by giving her a name, but as her leg was healing nicely and she'd filled out a little with proper food, I figured I should call her something other than Cat. But with my head awash with facts and figures from a tricky planning case, the best I could come up with was Jane. Yes, I'd seen that Marvel movie far too many times.

Still, eBay had come up with the goods once more, and she had a Great Dane-sized cage to recuperate in, a covered litter tray, a soft blanket, and matching food and water bowls decorated with little fish. Best of all, when I went to collect her, the deep purrs as I scritched her head made the four-figure vet bill worth every penny.

The taxi driver chatted to me on the way home, and when I told him the story, he even offered to carry the travel basket upstairs for me. Normally I'd have refused, but visions of Dane popping out of his flat to "help" saw me thanking the man politely as I held the outer door open. The last thing I needed was another uncomfortable conversation with my nearest neighbour.

"That was very kind of you," I said, slipping the driver a tip as I backed through my front door.

"No bother, ma'am. It's a real shame her owner didn't come forward."

Kind of, but as Cat snuggled on my lap through the rebooted *Ghostbusters* movie, I couldn't help smiling about the new addition. Loki seemed to like her too, while Thor was more interested in the salmon I'd bought them all for tea. Waitrose's finest organic wild-caught salmon, complete with a catnip garnish. Yes, crazy cat woman had arrived.

As did a wind-up mouse, a fluffy fish on a pole, and three kinds of kitty treats the next morning, stacked neatly beside my caramel macchiato and a double-chocolate muffin. Bloody Dane. He *had* been watching me when I arrived home yesterday, hadn't he? The mere thought made me want to install a rope ladder on my balcony to climb up to my flat, just to avoid his beady eyes. He may have seemed relatively normal, if a little eager, when I first met him, but rushing out to the twenty-four-hour Tesco to shop for cat accessories before I even woke up took him beyond dedicated and well into freak territory.

And worse, now that I needed to pop home each lunchtime for a few weeks to check on Cat, I'd have to run the gauntlet two extra times every day. Part of me wished I *was* renting the bloody flat because then I could have handed in my notice and run for the hills, but even the thought of that made anger bubble up inside me. This was my flat. My *home*. The idea of some weirdo driving me away made me want to throw something. No, not something. A caramel macchiato, at his head.

And things only got worse that evening. A knock at the door made me jump, because for once I was attempting to cook my own spaghetti rather than giving up and calling the Italian place down the street to deliver. Before I even looked through the peephole, the heaviness in my gut told me who my visitor was.

Luckily, the person who'd owned the flat before me had installed a security chain, and I made good use of it before I cracked the door open.

"What do you want, Dane?"

He held out a bottle of red and a bundle of pink feathers tied onto a length of purple string. "I thought I'd come over to meet your new cat, and we could have a nice drink while we're at it."

Why on earth would he think I wanted to do that? I racked my brains, desperately trying to work out what signals I'd given off that could possibly have said "invite yourself over and let's get tipsy," but came up with nothing.

"I'm busy this evening."

"Really? What with?"

Oh, how I longed to just tell him to get lost, but alone in a quiet corridor, the last thing I wanted was to make him angry. I wasn't small, but he stood two inches taller than me and I already knew he worked out.

"I have a conference call with some clients in New York in..." I made a show of looking at my watch. "Ten minutes."

His smile faded away. "Right. Tomorrow, then?"

"Actually, I'm out tomorrow evening."

Dane nodded to himself. "Ah, the art class?"

Stalker much? Had he followed me there? I spoke through clenched teeth. "Yes, my art class."

"Always was good with a paintbrush. Maybe I should join you?"

My last little bit of sanctuary, gone? "It's full at the moment."

"Well, make sure you let me know if a slot opens up."

"Sure." Right around the time Satan took up downhill skiing.

"And if you need anyone to check on the cats during the day, you only have to ask."

Give him a key to my flat? Seriously? No, just no.

Once I'd closed the door on Dane, I leaned back against it and slid down to my bottom. Why me? Was this my penance for thinking all those dirty thoughts about Joe? Someone above reminding me that I played for Misfits United rather than mixing it up in the Premier League? If that was the case, I'd rather die alone. Well, apart from the cats.

***

As usual, Marie was already seated when I got to class the next day. Two weeks of Joe left to go, and she'd got her paints out.

"Thought I'd go for colour this week. At least he doesn't have tan lines."

My eyes rolled of their own accord. "What does Andy think of all this?"

"He sees the funny side, and as long as I go home to him at night, he doesn't care. Hey, I even got him to pose nude for me this week, you know, for practice." She fished her phone out of her pocket. "Want to see?"

"No!"

"I was only going to show you my drawing, not actual photos."

"That's still weird."

She shrugged. "Whatevs. Hey, speaking of weird, is that guy still bugging you? The gym guy?"

"This morning he brought me a s'mores frappuccino, a gift box of handmade cat treats, and a beginner's set of watercolour paints."

"That's...that's, uh, sweet?"

"It's not sweet. It's freaky. He knows I come to art class but I've never mentioned it, and he knew I'd got another cat within a day, even though I didn't tell a soul in my building. Either he was watching from the window as I got out of the cab, or he spied on me through the security viewer in his door."

"Okay, that's not so sweet. Does he do this to anyone else?"

"I don't know. Apart from him, none of the neighbours ever speak to me. I've only seen the man who lives on the other side half a dozen times since I moved in. I think he works away a lot."

"Maybe you should tell the police if he keeps watching you?"

"Tell them what? That my odd neighbour keeps leaving me unwanted gifts? I doubt I'd be a priority."

"But if something happened, at least it would be on record."

The thought of "something" happening made my chest seize. "Please, can we not talk about this?"

Marie pasted on a perky smile. "Right, okay. So, you got another cat? I thought you never wanted more than two? What's it called?"

"Er, Cat?"

Marie shook her head and laughed. "You can't keep calling it Cat."

"I know, but I haven't felt very inspired."

"Brad Kitt? Catrick Swayze? Fuzz Lightyear? Chairman Meow?"

"She's a girl."

"Smiley Cyrus? Tuna Catserole?"

I scrunched my nose up.

"You don't like any of those?"

"I'll keep thinking."

"Your loss. So what's the story? Where did you buy her?"

"I didn't." I told Marie the gist of the situation, carefully leaving out any mention of Joe. "And now I've got to know Cat, I don't think I can bear to take her to a shelter."

"Oh, you'll keep her. That's the sort of person you

are. Have you got photos?"

Only about three hundred. I scrolled through a few on my phone and showed Marie my favourite, where Cat lay on my lap as I watched TV with Loki next to her.

"So cute!" Marie nudged me and jerked her head to the door. "And speaking of cute... Our favourite art model is here."

CHAPTER 9

YES, JOE WAS there, and yes, cute didn't even begin to do him justice, but this week I couldn't help noticing the slight hunch of his shoulders and the dark shadows under his eyes. When he caught me looking and gave me a half smile, I didn't want to draw him, I wanted to tuck him into bed and bring him a mug of cocoa.

But when I glanced at the rest of the class, nobody else seemed to share my thoughts, judging by the poised pencils and the murmurs of approval when Joe dropped the sheet from around his waist.

"If you could just lie there on the sheet," Delores told him, flitting around like a rainbow on acid. "Lean back against the pillows. No, move your head to the right... Good, that's perfect."

"She's right about that last bit," Marie whispered. "Hot damn. I swear he's grown an inch since last week."

Even with the good bits on show, I found myself drawn to Joe's face. At one point, his eyes flicked in my direction and I summoned up the courage to smile, but the instant after our gazes locked, he fixed his eyes on the ceiling and studiously ignored me. As the minutes turned into an hour, I began to wonder if I did something to upset him last week. Were cracked polystyrene tiles really so interesting he couldn't even acknowledge my existence?

"Those hands are a bit on the small side," Delores said, coming over to appraise my work. "The length of the hand and wrist together should equal the height of his head, remember?"

I nodded. My carefully measured proportions had gone out the window as I kept glancing back to Joe's face. The poor guy looked as if he was struggling to keep his eyes open. Part of me wanted the class to be over so he could go home and get some sleep, and the rest of me longed to sit here forever, drinking in the man I spent every spare moment obsessing over. Good grief, I'd turned into the female equivalent of Dane, hadn't I? Except without the weird coffee and cat treats.

And right now, I only had one hundred and thirty-seven minutes left in which to legitimately ogle Joe. My pencil strokes took on a new urgency as this week's class drew to an end, but even though I carried on drawing as Joe walked off to change, I still hadn't managed to finish to my satisfaction. There was so much more I needed to add—the hint of stubble on his chin, the definition in his arm muscles, that tattoo I wanted to trace with my tongue.

"Wow," Marie said as she leaned over to look at my work. "You've got his face exactly right."

A grin crept over my lips. The face. That was the part of him I wanted to remember most. Yes, he had the physique of a fitness model, but I could find a dozen similar bodies to drool over on Google. Nothing would replace his kind eyes and that strong jaw.

"I still need to fill the rest of the detail in."

She pointed at his naughty bits. "And you could add

an inch or two there."

"Enough! Do you ever stop thinking with your nether regions?"

"Not often, and speaking of nether regions, as you so delicately put it, Andy's waiting at home."

A giggle escaped. "Well, enjoy yourself."

"I will, don't worry. Have you got time to meet for a coffee next week, or are you working late every day?"

"I'll make time. At least if I'm out, Dane won't be able to invite himself around again."

"I still think you should go to the police. Whatever you do, don't let him in."

"Don't worry, I've got no intention of that. My security chain is staying firmly on."

"Call me if he does anything more, yeah?"

"Okay."

"Promise?" Marie waved as she headed for the door, clutching her art case.

"Promise."

I set about cleaning my mess up, and once I'd put away my pencils, I went to retrieve last week's painting, now dry, from the cupboard. Seeing it again, I decided it was better than I remembered. Seven months ago, I'd never have been able to capture Joe's likeness like that, but pushing myself to come here every week had paid dividends. Far more than those flipping exercise classes. If I'd stuck with them, I'd probably have pulled a hamstring—if I hadn't died of embarrassment first.

I ran a fingernail along the edge of painted Joe's jawline, resisting the urge to trace lower, lower. Even on canvas, he looked damn hot.

And so unavailable.

Which was why when his husky voice sounded

behind me, I jumped half a metre in the air and dropped the damn painting on my foot. The corner of the wooden frame hit my instep, and I hopped a couple of steps then nearly fell over. *Oh, well done, Cate. You're doing a marvellous job of looking cool and sophisticated.*

"Shit—are you okay?" Joe asked.

I waved a hand, aiming for nonchalance and failing miserably.

"Oh, fine, just fine."

Not only was my foot throbbing like hell, when Joe stooped to pick up my painting, the corner was bashed in and last week I'd been more focused on his naughty bits than his face. He raised an eyebrow as he held the canvas out to me.

"Delores says it's important to focus on different aspects of a subject so we develop our skills."

His smile turned into a chuckle. "Still need to work on your proportions, though."

My eyes dropped involuntarily to his crotch. "No, I don't think so."

The chuckle morphed into a full-blown laugh and then a yawn. "Pretty sure I know what size I am."

Please, no, I couldn't have a conversation about his dick, especially when I knew what size he was too. Instead, I made a big show of arranging my art supplies in my bag, but when I put out my hand for the painting, he shook his head.

"I'll help you carry your stuff. Do you have another bag for this? Otherwise I'll get strange looks carrying a naked picture of myself along the pavement."

"I'll put it in my portfolio case, but honestly, you don't have to help. I'll be okay."

"I'm going the same way as you up to the traffic lights."

This man was too damn sweet, and a little shiver ran through me at the thought of spending a few more minutes with him.

"Are you sure? You look so tired today."

"Didn't sleep so well the last few nights." He yawned again, and this time I joined in. "Dinner and bed are called for."

"You haven't eaten yet either?"

"Came straight from work. How's the cat?"

"She's doing well. I picked her up from the vet yesterday, and she's recuperating in my flat."

"No luck finding the owner?"

"Nothing. I put posters up all over the place, but the only person to call was a guy wanting to know if there was a reward for taking her off my hands."

"Arsehole. I saw the posters. Should have helped you with those."

"It didn't take long. My assistant at work laminated them all, so I only had to stick them up."

Joe held the door open for me, and I ducked under his arm into the cool night air. Even though it was August, the temperature still dropped into the low teens at night. Joe hadn't worn a jacket this week, and as we set off, I noticed the goosebumps on his arms.

"Cold?" I asked.

"Chilled off since earlier."

"You didn't bring a jacket?"

"Haven't got around to buying a new one yet."

He only had one jacket and he gave it to the cat? And how could he not have had time to buy a new one? There were shops everywhere in London, and ordering on the internet only took a minute. Unless... Last week at the vet he'd mentioned being short of cash. What if he couldn't afford a new jacket? Guilt welled up inside me as I remembered how he paid the cab fare then bought me dinner.

Should I offer again to pay him back? I soon dismissed that idea—he'd most likely be offended. But I couldn't let it go. Inspiration struck when we passed the café we'd eaten in last week, and I stopped outside the brightly lit window.

Joe carried on for a couple of steps before turning back. "What's up?"

"I'm hungry, and it's my turn to buy dinner."

"You don't need to do that."

"Aren't you peckish? I'm starving. I ran out of time for lunch again, and I forgot to order groceries."

He looked through the window and then down the street before he answered. "I'll buy you dinner."

No, no, no. That wasn't my intention at all. "I owe you for last week."

"You don't owe me anything."

"Fine, I want to buy you dinner as a thank you for helping me."

"It doesn't feel right."

"We're in the twenty-first century. Equal opportunities and all that. Women can buy dinner now, you know." Good grief, were we having our first argument as...what? Were we even friends?

Joe looked away for a few seconds then sighed. "Okay."

"Good."

He reached out a hand. "Am I still allowed to open the door for you?"

"I can live with that."

CHAPTER 10

THE WIZENED OLD lady from last week was standing behind the counter, doing a crossword puzzle, and she grinned when she saw Joe. Who wouldn't?

"Same as last week, love?" she asked.

Joe looked at me and raised his eyebrows.

"Yes, please." I hadn't contracted salmonella or anything, so I figured it was safe.

Not content with opening the door, Joe pulled out my chair as well. The whole chivalry thing felt odd to me. The accountant had prided himself on working for an equal opportunities firm, and looking back, he'd been a prick to everyone, male or female. Being treated like a princess by Joe may have been old fashioned, but I kind of liked it.

"So, the operation went okay?" he asked.

"Mr. Fraser put a plate in, and now she's got to wear a cast for six weeks until the bone knits back together. But she can still hop around pretty quickly."

"Does she get on okay with your cats?"

"Touch wood." I pressed my fingers onto the edge of the scarred wooden chair then grimaced as they stuck to a piece of chewing gum. Delightful. I resisted the urge to run screaming and wiped them on a napkin while Joe got up to fetch our cups of tea. "Loki's taken quite a shine to her."

"Sounds like you have too. What did you call her?"

"Uh, Cat? I haven't thought of a proper name yet. Marie made some suggestions, but the best one was Smiley Cyrus."

Joe choked on a mouthful of tea then grimaced. "You shouldn't have told me that while I was drinking."

"Sorry."

"Smiley Cyrus? Seriously? That was the best?"

"I could have called her Chairman Miaow."

He shook his head in disbelief. "Does Marie have kids?"

"No, why?"

"I was just curious as to what she'd call them."

"I'm fairly sure neither of us want to know. Although when I first met her, her sister had just given birth to a girl and Marie was trying to convince her to name the baby Dublin after where she conceived. Well, it was either Dublin or Buncrana, but thankfully Marie's sister saw sense and went with Sophie."

That got a proper smile from Joe, the first I'd seen, and my heart did a little skip. Handsome didn't even begin to cover it.

"If you've already got Thor and Loki, how about another name from Norse mythology?"

"I'm not so hot on Norse mythology."

"Frigg, Sif, Idun, Beyla, Embla. I'd suggest Freya, but that's my sister and naming a cat after her would feel odd."

"You have a sister? How old?"

"Twenty-two. She's at uni in Oxford."

"At *the* Oxford? Or Oxford Brookes?"

"The Oxford."

I could hear the pride in Joe's voice, and it was

deserved. I knew from experience how difficult it was to get into that university.

"Ooh, I went there. Which college?"

"Oriel."

"Just along the road from me—I went to Univ."

"I always figured you were smart."

"Maybe, but I really wanted to go to art college. Studying law was my father's idea. Not that I totally regret doing it, because working at Berkeley, Rogers and Smyth means I have a very comfortable life, even if it's a bit dull, but sometimes I just wish that I'd abandoned all the boring case studies in my first year and travelled the world, painting, because... Listen to me, I'm rambling on about myself again." A huge breach of dating etiquette, even though this *wasn't a date*. "Tell me about you."

Joe chuckled as the lady brought our food over. "Talk as much as you like. I'd rather hear about you."

"I'm not that interesting."

He shrugged. "You have any brothers or sisters?"

"No, I'm an only child."

And so it went on. We got to the end of the meal, and I realised Joe had neatly sidestepped every question about himself, while I'd told him most of my life's history. He'd have done well in a courtroom. As the lady took our plates away, I decided to have one last try.

"Did you have any pets growing up? Apart from the tabby cat?"

He looked surprised I'd remembered, but recalling every fact was my job and I knew precious few about Joe.

"No, no other pets unless you count the snail I

brought to dinner when I was five. Mum evicted him fairly fast. That reminds me, we never did name your cat."

Aaaaaaand we were back to me. I couldn't help sighing. "No, we didn't. I'm not sure she's a Frigg or a Sif, but Beyla would suit her."

"Beyla, then?"

I nodded as I went up to the counter to pay, and by the time I'd finally got my own smile from the lady because I left a decent tip, Joe was waiting by the door with my portfolio case.

"I can take that. We'll be parting ways in fifty yards."

He shook his head. "It's late. I'll walk you home again."

I cursed myself for remembering my own jacket this week because that meant Joe didn't offer me his arm again. He just walked close enough to me to make my heart beat faster and my skin prickle. I managed not to blabber on and instead tried my best to relax in the presence of a man who I longed to spend more time with. He may not have had the money of the accountant or the pedigree of the viscount I dallied with briefly at university, but he made my knickers damp in a way neither of the others had.

All too soon, we arrived at Heron Court, and I glanced up at the windows next to mine. One was lit, and even though I couldn't see Dane's face, I could feel him watching. The delicious heat I felt from Joe was replaced by a chill creeping through my veins.

"Uh, do you want to come in for coffee?" Oh, hell. Could I sound any more cheesy and desperate? "I mean, I thought you might like to see Beyla?"

I kept my fingers crossed behind my back, partly because I didn't want Joe to leave but mostly because I didn't want to walk up to my apartment alone. All I needed at this time of night was to be accosted by Dane as I tried to get my front door open.

Joe took a step back and I thought he was going to refuse, but then he nodded. "Yeah. I wouldn't mind coffee."

The temperature of the lift rose a few degrees with Joe's proximity, and that scene from *Fifty Shades of Grey* where Christian kissed Ana flitted through my mind. Okay, it didn't so much flit as broadcast an open invitation should Joe fancy doing the same thing, but he maintained a polite distance, holding my portfolio case in front of him. As we disembarked, the motion-activated lights flicked on in the hallway, and I half hoped Dane was watching. My middle finger did too, and I resisted the childish urge to hold it up at his peephole. Prick.

"What the hell is that?" Joe asked, pointing towards my door.

"Uh, I have no idea."

We walked closer, and a loud groan escaped my lips. A scratching post. Dane had left a three-storey bloody scratching post, complete with a box of chocolates and a note on the top level. I tore the paper out of the envelope.

Cate,

I'm leaving early tomorrow, so I brought you chocolate tonight instead of your morning coffee.

Dane x

Arrrgh! I kicked the scratching post then swore when my toe throbbed. Joe leaned over my shoulder and read the note before I screwed it up and threw it on the floor.

"What's wrong?"

"It's my bloody neighbour. He keeps leaving me all these gifts I don't want."

"A scratching post? He's put some thought into that. What did he say when you asked him to stop?"

"Uh..." Could it really be that simple? "I haven't exactly asked him to stop. Mostly I just try to ignore him."

Joe picked up the scratching post in his free hand so I could get to the front door. "Well, try asking. Some men need to hear it straight."

"I will. I'll speak to him tomorrow. Or whenever I see him next." The thought of knocking on his door scared me, like if I went near him voluntarily, I might get sucked through a portal into hell when it opened. "Well, this is me."

I motioned into my hallway, thankful I always kept it clean and tidy. Well, apart from that little pile of cat puke in the corner. Dammit! What had Thor been eating? Because it was always Thor who threw up, never Loki. A whiff of frappuccino drifted up to me. Tell me Thor hadn't licked it out of the sink? Shit.

Joe held up the scratching post and my portfolio case. "What do you want me to do with these?"

What I wanted to do was laugh at the sheer awfulness of the situation. Not that I was any good at the seduction thing, but introducing the guy I had the hots for to my home with cat vomit and a gift from my stalker probably came under "what not to do" in the handbook.

"Uh, just put them anywhere. I'd better clear up

the, uh..." I closed my eyes and pointed at Thor's efforts, hoping that when I opened them again, it would all have been a bad dream.

But no, the stinking pile was still there, topped by, if I wasn't mistaken, a small marshmallow.

"Do you need a hand?"

"No!" Good grief. "Cat...Beyla's in the spare bedroom. Second door on the right."

I wanted to cry as I cleared up. Okay, I did cry. Just a couple of tears, but they symbolised everything that went wrong in my life. The only thing I was good at was work, and no matter what I said to Dane, I didn't particularly enjoy the hours I put in at Berkeley, Rogers and Smyth. Work was like being stuck in a hamster wheel for twelve hours a day with no way out.

I finished sponging the beige carpet while Thor watched, and I prayed it wouldn't stain.

"What's wrong with kitty treats, you little monster?"

He just tilted his head to one side as if to say, "What do you expect when you're not here all day?" then stalked off.

And now I needed to face Joe again. He saved me the trouble of going to find him by walking through to the kitchen with Beyla in his arms, purring away. Guess I wasn't the only one who liked him.

"She seems happy," he said. "Is she eating?"

"Everything in sight, but the vet said not to let her put on weight too quickly."

"Sensible."

The awkward silence did nothing for my nerves, and I rushed to fill it. "Shall I make that coffee now?"

"You know what? It's late. Me staying probably isn't

a great idea."

He wasn't talking about coffee, was he? He was talking about everything that coffee at the end of an evening stood for. He'd taken a good look at me and my life, and it didn't measure up to his expectations.

Tears threatened again as I held my arms out for Beyla and forced some cheer into my voice. "You're right. I'm sure you've got an early start tomorrow, as do I."

"I can find my own way out." He handed over the cat then surprised me by cupping my face in his hand and running a thumb over my cheekbone. "Goodnight, Cate. Look after yourself."

"I will," I whispered, but he was already gone, leaving me alone with the ghost of his touch and a heart that had no right to feel as broken as it did.

CHAPTER 11

LIGHTS FROM THE traffic below played across the ceiling as I lay awake, the glimmers casting eerie shadows from the Victorian ceiling mouldings. Yes, I needed to sleep, but it eluded me as yet another embarrassing evening with Joe replayed in my mind.

The man remained an enigma. A hot enigma, tonight wrapped up in the same soft jeans as last week but with a white T-shirt instead of black. And I was still confused. He'd seemed interested in me in the café, enough to ask me all about my childhood and my time at Oxford, and then he'd accepted my invitation for coffee before backing out. Did he really only want to check on the cat? Or having seen me in my natural environment, did he realise he'd made a huge mistake? I glanced down at myself in the light from the street lamp outside, resplendent in the oversized *Toy Story* T-shirt I wore as a nightie. No, he hadn't made a mistake. What on earth had made me believe I stood a chance with him? How had I let myself get so wrapped up in the moment?

Stupid, Cate. Stupid.

With Dane mercifully absent the next morning, I took a wander down to Starbucks for a double espresso in an attempt to wake myself up. When I gave my name and spelled it out of habit, the perky barista gave me a funny look.

"Doesn't your boyfriend usually buy you something fancier?" she asked, ginger curls bobbing around her face.

"Boyfriend? I don't have a boyfriend." The realisation dawned on me. "Do you mean Dane?"

"I don't know his name. About your height, brown hair, runs a recruitment business?"

"He's not my boyfriend."

"Well, he says you're his girlfriend."

"Perhaps you misheard him?"

"No, I don't think so. Every morning, he says something like, 'My girlfriend's still in bed,' or, 'I wore Cate out last night, so she's still sleeping.'"

That... That... I didn't even have words. It took a few seconds for me to unclench my teeth. "Dane is *not* my boyfriend. He's a delusional freak who lives down the hall and buys me coffee I don't drink almost every morning. I don't even like frappuccinos."

"Okay, that's weird."

"Tell me about it."

"Uh, is there anything I can do? Like, I could refuse to serve him?"

"No, don't bother. I'm planning to talk to him about it."

"Are you sure that's a good idea?"

"No, but I still need to do it."

"Maybe you should go to the police?"

She was the second person to suggest that, but even though I knew a handful of cops from work, I worried about wasting their time on such a trivial matter. Besides, Dane hadn't done anything but buy me gifts and make inappropriate comments—strange, but hardly a crime.

"No, I'll speak to him first. But if neither of us comes in for coffee next week, perhaps you could ask the police to pop around and check for a body?"

I'd made a joke out of it, but she nodded solemnly. "I'll do that."

***

To make a bad day worse, my mobile rang the instant I sat down at my desk. I let it go to voicemail, but a minute later Reggie buzzed through with the news that my mother was on line two.

"Can you tell her I've gone out?"

"You know she'll call back."

"What if you said I'd gone on holiday? One of those treks through the rainforest where there's no phone signal?"

"Remember last time you did that and she called the embassy in Ecuador to check you were okay?"

"Fine, I'll speak to her. But you'd better interrupt with an emergency pretty damn quickly."

It wasn't that I didn't love my mother. It was more that she had very specific ideas about how I should be living my life, and most of them weren't compatible with mine. Take the cats, for example. I'd lost count of the number of times she'd told me that a single woman's first cat was a substitute for a husband, and the second stood in for a child. What would she say if she found I'd added a third? While Daddy was proud when I made junior partner, Mother tutted, told me I'd made my point, and said it was high time I settled down and gave her grandchildren.

"Hi, Mum."

"Catherine, it's been over a month since you called. I know we're in the technological age, but emailing isn't good enough."

Maybe not, but she couldn't put me on the spot in an email. "Sorry, I've been busy."

"How is your verruca, anyway? Did the surgery go well?"

Fine, I admit it, I was hopeless at making up excuses. The verruca story came out of desperation coupled with a chiropodist's advert on the billboard I happened to be walking past at the time.

"Uh, it's gone now."

"Good, good. Then you'll be able to circulate properly at your father's birthday party in two weeks."

"He's having a party? He never has a party."

"It's a surprise. We can't let his sixtieth pass without a celebration."

She hadn't told him? My father and I might have had differences of opinion over the years, but one thing we did agree on was that Mother's parties were to be avoided at all costs. He'd snuck out with a bottle of red wine on my eighteenth, and we'd shared it behind the potting shed while the crowd Mother invited noshed on canapés and discussed my future in the house.

I needed to return the favour.

"I'll put it in my diary."

"Excellent, excellent. You can bring Bruce. I've told all the ladies from tennis about him."

Shit. Bruce. The accountant. It may have slipped my mind to tell Mother we were no longer an item. "Uh, we broke up."

"Oh, Catherine." The disappointment in her voice

was all too evident. "What did you do?"

I hooked the phone against my shoulder and gripped the edge of my desk to stop myself from throwing something. Why did she always assume it was my fault? It was the same with the viscount, and he'd cheated on me.

"We just grew apart." It was better than admitting he'd told me I was too dull then changed his Facebook status the next day to say he was in a relationship with his secretary. Who was a size bloody eight.

"It's inconvenient, but I'm sure I can sort something out. Verity Barrington-Foster's son's single at the moment. I'm sure he would oblige if Verity asked him."

"I can come on my own."

"Don't be ridiculous, darling."

If Verity's son was anything like his mother, I'd be behind the potting shed with vodka, not wine. "I'm actually seeing someone new."

"Another accountant? A lawyer?"

A figment of my imagination? Hurry up, Reggie. "It's only been a few weeks, and I don't want to jinx things by talking about it."

"Never mind. We can find out all about him when you come for the party."

"He might be busy that day."

"I'm sure when you explain how important it is, he'll rearrange his schedule. Your father only turns sixty once."

Reggie stuck his head around the door and called loud enough for my mother to hear, "Stewart Doyle's on line one."

"Sorry, Mum, got to go. There's a client wanting to

speak to me."

"Will you be coming up to stay the night before the party?"

"No, just on the day."

"It starts at seven. Don't be late."

Marvellous, now I had to add finding a boyfriend onto my to-do list. A vision of the two men in my life popped into my head. Well, I'd screwed things up royally with Joe, but surely Dane would accompany me if I asked? I choked back a laugh. Yeah, right. I'd rather walk down Oxford Street naked than take Dane home to meet my parents. Maybe I could try one of those escort agencies? Rent a man for the evening? It wasn't as if he'd have to keep up the pretence for long—after her fourth or fifth martini, my mother wouldn't even recognise him.

I tapped a message to Marie.

Me: I might need to hire a man for a party. Any ideas?

Two seconds later.

Marie: Full service?

I spat a mouthful of coffee across my desk and hastily blotted it up. It was too early for Marie's dirty mind.

Me: No! A few hours at my father's birthday party, all clothes to remain on.

Marie: Hmmm, let me have a think...

***

As I walked across the grounds of Heron Court that evening, I was so busy worrying about the logistics of passing a gigolo off as my boyfriend, I didn't notice

Dane hidden behind the bouquet of flowers in the entrance hall until it was too late.

"Cate, you're home early. I thought you were working late this week?"

Mental note: never, ever leave the office at seven again. "I'm feeling tired."

"Maybe an evening off cooking would help? I can take you out for dinner."

"I just want to go to bed."

Dane's creepy smile grew wider. "I thought you'd never ask. Here, I got you these."

I sneezed as the lily pollen got up my nose. "Dane, this has got to stop."

"What's got to stop?"

"The coffee, the gifts, the following me around."

He laid a hand on my arm, and when I took a step back, he took a step forward. "If you're thinking like that, it means I still need to try harder. All women enjoy being spoiled."

"Not this one."

"It's sad that you've been conditioned to think that way. You deserve the attention."

"But I don't *want* the attention."

"Every woman likes to feel desired. It's flattering."

"But—"

"I know you got ditched last night, and you don't need to worry about that. Yes, I was a little upset you chose to invite another man into your home, but he didn't stay for long, so I've got over it. And his brush-off doesn't make you any less attractive to me."

I shoved the flowers back at Dane and ran for the stairs. The prickly feeling of his gaze on my back made me want to throw up, and I couldn't wait for the elevator. The instant I got into my apartment, I bolted the door closed and burst into tears. Too much. These last few days had been too much. I held my breath as Dane's footsteps sounded on the landing outside. A pause, a rustle as he set the flowers down outside my door, and then they carried on into his flat.

So much for Joe's idea of asking Dane to back off. I knew now that would never happen. My eyes stung as I wiped a hand across them, and Loki wandered over to see what the fuss was about.

"It's all right, little one. Just human drama. I'll think of a plan, don't worry."

Don't worry. That's what Dane said to me earlier, and I wasn't worried—I was bloody terrified.

Chapter 12

TWO MORE HOURS. Two more hours of Joe, and after last week I doubted class would be followed by weak tea and an all-day breakfast. Not that I needed breakfast. After our little chat, Dane had upped the ante and brought me pastries from Patisserie Valerie every single day. If I saw another croissant, I'd probably be sick. Not only that, I suspected he'd started buying cat toys in bulk, because Thor, Loki, and Beyla had enough furry mice to start their own pet shop and Thor in particular was in a perpetual state of euphoria because of all the catnip he'd been eating.

"I got what you asked for," Marie whispered, handing over a folder full of printouts as if they were contraband.

I peered inside. Wow. These gigolos weren't shy about letting it all hang out, were they?

"Leo's my favourite because of the eyes," Marie told me, somehow managing to keep a straight face. "But he's only eight inches. If you want nine, Warren's the best of the bunch, but he's so cut, you might hurt yourself on those muscles."

"Which part about them keeping their clothes on didn't you understand?"

"You weren't serious about that, were you?"

"Yes!"

"But it's been months. There's only so much a girl can do with a Rampant Rabbit. You do have a Rabbit, don't you?"

In my nightstand, and plenty of spare batteries, but no way was I admitting that in the middle of an art class. "Marie, stop it."

"Just fingers then?" She waggled an eyebrow.

"Please..." Joe would be out any second, and I couldn't be having this conversation.

"I know none of them are as hot as you know who." Her eyes flicked towards the empty dais. "But I asked around and all of those guys have a good reputation."

"I'll give them careful consideration, I promise."

Finally, she relented. "How's the cat?"

"Doing well. She's getting around pretty quickly with her cast on."

"Is that guy still bothering you?"

"Mmm hmm."

"Cate, look at me."

"What?"

"How bad is it?"

"Worse than ever," I whispered.

"You need to tell somebody. Get a restraining order or something."

"It's embarrassing. And besides, he hasn't actually done anything apart from buying me presents and following me a bit."

"Yet. He hasn't done anything yet. Tell the police, please. Do you want me to come with you?"

"I'll think about it, I promise."

The chatter around the class stopped as Joe walked out, followed by Delores, who'd also gone into mourning about the end of Joe's modelling stint, it seemed, dressed as she was in a black muumuu with silver trim. And she'd gone with a matching sheet for Joe, who didn't even look in my direction as she arranged him in a kneeling position angled towards one side of the room.

Not a glance, not a smile. Guess I knew where I stood.

My sadness came out on the page as I drew a couple of quick studies then a detailed sketch of Joe's face. I checked out Marie's canvas and predictably she was painting him full-frontal in all his technicolour glory, but I cared about the man, not his manhood. Even though he'd hurt me, I still cared.

Twice I caught him biting the corner of his lip, and it struck me that he didn't look particularly happy either. But if last week's meal was anything to go by, even if I asked him what was wrong, he wouldn't tell. It struck me that we were both messed up, but if he didn't share, I couldn't help him.

One hundred and twenty minutes flew by, and before I knew it, Delores was thanking Joe for his time. The class clapped politely as he wrapped the sheet around his waist, and then he walked away.

"Do you want me to walk home with you?" Marie asked as I packed up my stuff. "Andy'll understand."

"I'll be okay."

The dumb part of me still held out hope that Joe might hang around to talk to me, but deep inside I knew he wouldn't. He'd gone. All the dreams I'd had about him were destined to remain exactly that. Dreams.

"It's no bother, honestly. Just a few extra stops on the Tube and I haven't seen the cats for ages."

"I'm not sure..."

My indecision was interrupted by Delores, who wandered out from the back room and held out a package wrapped in silver paper to me, one eyebrow raised.

"Joe asked me to give you this. He didn't bring anyone else a gift, so you must have made quite an impression."

"For me?"

She pointed at my name, written in the corner in black pen.

"Open it, open it!" Marie said, clapping her hands together.

It felt like it should be a private moment, but I couldn't refuse, not with both of them staring at me. I tore the paper off and found a cream-and-silver photo frame, vintage style to match my flat. And that wasn't all. A card slotted into the front bore a single red rose, and I opened it to read the message.

Cate,

You're too talented to hide away and too sweet to be alone. Be brave and face the world, and don't let anybody crush your dreams.

Joe.

"OMG!" Marie squealed. "He likes you! He really likes you."

"That's the sweetest thing I've ever read," Delores added.

I had to swallow the lump in my throat before I could speak. "Where is he?"

"He left, sweetie. A couple of minutes ago."

Now what? I didn't have his number, I didn't have a clue where he worked, hell, I didn't even know his surname. All I knew was that he went in a different direction to me at the traffic lights up the road.

"I should thank him. I need to thank him," I muttered.

"Go." Delores gave me a little push towards the door. "He turned left. You can catch him if you hurry."

Marie gave me a bigger shove. "I'll sort out your stuff. Now bloody run!"

So I did, cursing my decision to wear heels rather than trainers today. Outside, a fine drizzle misted the air, and my hair was soon plastered to my face as rain mixed with sweat. His card said not to let anybody crush my dreams? Well, the person who wrote it had just tried his best to do exactly that. Sod it, I'd tell him how I felt. There was every chance he'd stomp on my heart entirely, but at least I wouldn't always be left wondering "what if?"

Three hundred yards, two hundred, then I was at the traffic lights and there was no sign of him. Four directions, one chance. Which way should I go?

I spotted a homeless man watching me from a shop doorway, knees drawn up inside his sleeping bag.

"Excuse me? I'm looking for a blond man who walked past here a few minutes ago. About six feet tall. I don't suppose you can tell me which direction he went?"

The man pointed wordlessly down the street opposite, and I fumbled a ten-pound note from my purse and dropped it into his lap.

"Thanks!" I said.

Then I was off again, jogging along the road, until suddenly I wasn't anymore. Words my mother would have had a fit at flew from my lips as I fell on one knee, taking a layer of skin off and ruining my tights.

"Dammit." The heel of my left shoe was firmly wedged in a crack in the pavement, and when I tried to pull it out, the sodding thing snapped off entirely. Now tears mixed in with the sweat and rain.

But I'd come this far, so I kicked my dignity into the gutter along with my other shoe and took off along the pavement barefoot, splashing through the puddles and grimacing when I trod in something squishy.

Then I saw him up ahead, and my voice came out as a strangled cry. "Joe!"

He turned, eyes widening as I performed my coup de grâce—stubbing my toe on a loose paving slab as I tripped over and landed in his arms.

Well, it never happened like this in the movies.

"Cate? What are you doing here?"

"You left. You left without a word and you gave me such a sweet gift."

"You shouldn't have come. It's raining."

"But I needed to thank you. So, uh, thank you." Nope, this wasn't awkward at all. "Why did you leave?"

He leaned down and rested his forehead on mine. "Because I'm no good for you."

"And you decided that all by yourself? No input from me?"

"You don't know me."

"Then let me get to know you."

"Please, just leave now. It's best for both of us."

"No." I took half a step back and folded my arms. "You may not like me in the same way I like you, but I think you're lonely and so am I. We could both use a friend, so you're stuck with me."

He tucked a strand of wet hair behind my ear. "No,

Catie."

"Catie?"

"Cate's too harsh for you. In my head, you've always been Catie."

In his head? "You've been thinking about me?"

"Of course I have. Every moment since I first laid eyes on you."

"Then why are you running away?"

"Because I'm nothing." The way he said that, I knew he truly believed it. "Catie, please. You'll get a chill."

"Nope, I'm staying here." Wherever "here" was. I looked past Joe for the first time, taking in the railings of the old church to the side of us, gravestones glistening in the moonlight. A faded sign told me everyone was welcome at St. Jude's, and smaller letters next to an arrow underneath told me where the homeless shelter was. Right down the alley where Joe had been walking.

"Why are you going to the homeless shelter?"

He let out a long sigh. "Because they let me have a bed when there's one free, and the nuns watch my stuff when I'm at work."

"You're homeless?" Fuck, fuck, fuck. Sorry, Mother. Of all the secrets I'd expected him to have, that one never even entered my mind.

He shrugged. "It's not that bad really."

"Will you get a bed here tonight?"

"Not this late. They always fill up by the middle of the evening."

"So the nights you stayed out with me, you slept on the streets? And last week, that's why you were so tired?"

"There were people who needed the spaces more

than me." He took a step back. "Don't look at me that way. Anything but that."

"Look at you what way?"

"With pity." He dropped his voice so low I could hardly hear. "I didn't want the last look I got from you to be pity."

What should I do? *What should I do?* He might see pity, but what I felt was panic. All my fantasies about a hot gym trainer with a messy bachelor pad where we may possibly have had rampant sex on the sofa came crashing down, replaced by...what? Joe was still Joe— kind, gentle, sweet, not to mention hotter than hell, just homeless. Mother would have a fit if she found out I'd fallen for a homeless person, or a filthy vagrant, as she called them whenever we passed one in the street. Because I had fallen for him, hadn't I? And money or no money, he was still the same damn person.

"I'm sorry. I didn't mean to. It's just a shock, I guess."

He gave a hollow laugh. "I can appreciate that. Do you want me to walk you back to the Tube station?" He glanced down at my feet. "Shit, what happened to your shoes?"

"They weren't so good for running."

"Catie, you're crazy, but in a good way. Come on, I'll find you a cab."

"I already told you, I'm sticking with you, so the only way I'm going in a cab is if you're in it with me. I've got a spare room, so you can sleep in it."

"Like I said, you're too damn sweet, but I can't do that."

"That's fine. I'll just get pizza delivered to whatever bench you decide we're sleeping on."

"You've got to stop this."

"Why? Give me one good reason why you can't stay in my flat tonight."

"Because I'd never want to fucking leave," he muttered, then straightened a little. "We need to be serious. Look, it's not just my living situation that's the problem here. It's your job."

Huh? "Why is me being a lawyer a problem? I don't turn into a ball-buster the moment I put on a suit. If you must know, I actually get really nervous whenever I go to court."

"You're a property lawyer. And part of the reason I ended up in this mess was because of a property problem, and I can't afford to pay my lawyer to carry on with the case at the moment. I never wanted you to think I was using you because of what you do."

"So you decided it would be kinder to walk away without even saying goodbye?"

"As I said, it seemed like the best decision."

"Well, speaking from—"

A dim light flicked on behind us, and a thin voice came out of the darkness. "Is everything okay out here?"

"Sister Agnes?"

"Joe? Is that you?"

"Yes, it's me. Everything's fine."

"We saved you some soup, and Mother Superior says you can stay in the dining hall tonight if you're leaving early tomorrow, since the weather's so bad."

"You're a saint, Agnes. I'll be inside in a minute."

She giggled. The nun bloody giggled. "You're a good man, Joe."

He was a good man. And he was also a stupid man

if he thought I was giving up on him.

"Someone once told me to be brave and face the world, and not to let anybody crush my dreams. So, here I am, facing my world. And the person who can crush my dreams is standing right in front of me, seeing as he's been parading through them every night for the past month."

Would he? Would he crush them?

"I don't know why you're nervous of the courtroom. You're impossible to argue with."

"I nearly always win, but that doesn't mean I don't want to throw up the whole time I'm in there." A bit like now, really.

He leaned back against the railings and let out a long breath. "Fine. I'll stay with you tonight because I don't want you standing out here in the cold with no shoes on. We can finish discussing this in the morning."

"Fine."

He rolled his eyes in a "good grief, what have I got into" sort of way. "I need to get my bag."

I smiled, the same way I did when the judge took my side. "I'll meet you in the cab."

CHAPTER 13

THE RAIN WAS falling harder when Joe jogged to the cab. I'd half expected him not to come, to hole up inside the shelter until I stomped in there and pointed out the error of his ways. But he opened the door and dumped a bag at my feet, the hefty kind backpackers used when they travelled across continents. His life. His life was in that one bag, and I thought of the entire cupboard I had at home filled with just stilettos and felt incredibly guilty.

"Still time to back out, Catie."

I folded my arms and gave him my "seriously?" face, and he settled back into the seat with a faint smile. Whether out of happiness or exasperation, I wasn't sure.

The cab only took five minutes to get to Heron Court, and when it pulled up in the car park outside, Joe reached for his wallet. Nice try.

"Lady already paid, mate," the cabbie told him.

"Score one to me, thank you very much."

Joe swung his bag onto his back, and I shrieked as he scooped me up and carried me towards the front door.

"Put me down! I'm too heavy."

"Nope. Score one to me, ball-buster."

He held me steady while I fumbled with my entry

fob, and he didn't let go all the way up in the lift and along the hallway. My feet only touched the floor when he put me down in front of my door to examine the package left outside.

"What is it?" he asked.

I took in the garish wrapping paper and the yellow bow. "Cat toys, chocolates, pastries. Take your pick. Or maybe a DVD. I got a box set of Harry Potter yesterday." And a note suggesting I might like to curl up on the sofa and watch them with Dane.

"That asshole's still bothering you?"

"I did what you suggested and asked him to stop, but he interpreted that as 'try harder.' He's probably watching us right now." I jerked my head towards the door at the end of the hall.

Joe narrowed his eyes then shoved the package through the open door with his foot. "Let him watch." He wrapped an arm around my waist and pressed his lips to my forehead before walking me backwards into my flat. And when I say walking, I mean he half carried me because my legs had turned to jelly.

"Thanks," I said, my words inadequate compared to the relief I felt at having some help with Dane.

"It's me who should be thanking you."

"You can put your bag in the spare room while I see what I've got in the fridge."

When Joe wandered through to the kitchen a few minutes later with Dane's package under one arm, I'd put on water to boil for spaghetti. If I got lucky, dinner might even turn out edible.

"What should I do with this?" Joe asked.

"Is it ticking?"

He gave it a shake and something clonked inside.

"Nope."

"Open it."

A coffee machine. Dane had bought me a coffee machine, complete with four hundred coffee pods in various sickly flavours and a bumper-sized bag of marshmallows. The note informed me it was so I'd think of him when I made my coffee, even if he wasn't there.

"This is getting ridiculous. And he's *always* there."

"I'll speak to him."

"I don't want you getting dragged into my mess."

"Well you're already involved in mine, so I can return the favour."

"Maybe if he saw you coming in tonight, that'll be enough. He noticed last time, because he made a snide comment about you ditching me when you left so quickly."

"Prick. He shouldn't be watching you like that."

"I know. I can't even go to the gym without him following."

"He joined the same gym?"

"We've got one here in the basement. It was one of the reasons I bought this flat, because I know I need to lose some weight, but I can't even use it. Then I get stressed and eat even more chocolate, and I'm already the biggest girl in the office and the only one who has a picture of her cats stuck to her computer rather than her boyfriend." And also the only one who sounded like a whiny teenager in front of the man she really, really liked.

"Some men prefer curves. Don't ever think you need to change the way you look because of what other people think."

A tear escaped, and I swiped it away. Why was I so emotional at the moment?

"What's wrong?"

"Nobody's ever said that to me before. Even my mother keeps telling me I need to drop a few pounds."

"Come here." He opened his arms, and I walked into them. There was nothing sexual about his hug, just the support I'd craved for so long. "You're beautiful, and don't let anybody tell you otherwise. I should have added that to my note, seeing as you're so fond of quoting my words back to me."

He drew away a little, and I held my breath with the crazy hope that he'd kiss me. But he didn't. With our lips so close together and his heart beating against my chest, I almost took the initiative myself, but fear of rejection held me back. I settled for the feel of his arms around my waist instead, at least until the water in the pan boiled over. Then I wriggled free and dived for the cooker.

"Oops. I'm not so good at making dinner."

"Want me to take over?"

"You can cook?"

"Not like a chef or anything, but I'm not bad."

"In that case, be my guest. Do you want a glass of wine?"

"Just one." He glanced back at me over his shoulder and winked. "Otherwise I might be tempted to take advantage of you."

In that case, he could have the whole bottle of Château La Fleur-Pétrus I'd been saving for a special occasion. Except that would be rubbing his nose in it a bit, moneywise. "Red or white?"

"I prefer red, but I'm not fussy."

Instead of the greasy spoon, this week I got the surreal situation of the object of my affections sitting opposite me at my breakfast bar, passing me the parmesan and topping up my glass when it got low. Guess he wasn't worried about me taking advantage of him. And now his big secret was out, he wasn't quite so closed off.

"How long have you been at the shelter?"

"About four or five months, on and off."

"I don't understand. You've got a job?"

"Living in London isn't cheap, and most of my money goes on my debts and my sister."

"Freya?"

"Freya. She's had problems since our mother died."

"Does your father help?"

"My father died before I was born, and Freya's was never on the scene."

"I'm sorry."

"Don't be. It's in the past, and if I dwell on it, I'll never move forwards."

His eyes took on a haunted look when he mentioned the past, and I had a feeling there were more skeletons lurking, but with the time approaching midnight and work the next day, I didn't fancy digging any further. Plus I worried it might scare Joe off. No, far better to take things slowly.

"Do you have to work tomorrow?" I asked.

"Eight till four."

"I usually start at eight too, but I rarely leave the office before six."

"You're in the City?"

"Yes. You?"

"East End."

Dinner felt a whole lot less awkward than in the café the previous two weeks, even though the circumstances were far from normal. And when Joe gave me a soft kiss on the cheek and took the door opposite mine for the spare room, I felt a pang of jealousy as Beyla toddled in there after him and clawed her way onto the bed. Lucky kitty.

But I also got a buzz as I crawled under my own duvet because when I woke in the morning, the first person I'd see would be Joe.

***

"You look tired. Didn't sleep well?" Joe asked.

No, I didn't. I'd woken at four, hot and bothered because I'd been dreaming of him, and made all the worse by the fact there were only two walls and four feet of corridor separating us. The stupid part of me wanted to creep into the spare bedroom and join him, but the sensible part overruled in favour of fingers. And despite having an orgasm that made my bed shake, I still hadn't got back to sleep again.

"Not really."

"I found a cafetière and ground coffee in the cupboard. Is that what you like to drink?"

"Black, no sugar."

"I also threw whatever Dane left outside the door down the sink." He wrinkled his nose. "Smelled fuckin' awful, and the barista wrote 'sorry' in the foam on the top. Do you know anything about that?"

"I may have mentioned the problem to her earlier in the week. He told her I was his girlfriend."

"Arsehole. You sure you don't want me to have a

word before I go?"

I'd thought about that while I was lying awake too, and I shook my head. "Irritating though he is, I still have to live next to him. I figure if he just sees you around a bit, he might back off." Especially if Joe looked like he did this morning, ready for work in loose shorts and a tight black T-shirt.

"You want me to come back?"

"Why do you sound so surprised? I said you could stay here."

"I assumed you meant for one night."

"Well, I didn't."

"It's not fair to just take over your spare room, especially when I can't afford to pay rent."

"Okay, fine. How about a non-monetary compensation arrangement?" Good grief, could I sound any more like a lawyer?

Joe's eyes widened. "I've never had a woman put it quite like that."

Oh, crap! Did he think I'd propositioned him? "I meant personal training in the gym downstairs. You can have the spare room in return for a couple of sessions a week."

Hopefully that wouldn't put too much of a dent in his pride.

"That doesn't seem like enough."

"Okay, fine. You want to do more? I need a man to accompany me to my father's birthday party before my mother finds me her own version of my perfect match."

He almost dropped the bag of coffee. "You want me to meet your parents?"

"The other option is for me to hire someone, but all the men Marie's found so far seem a little, uh, stripperish for what I need."

Joe burst out laughing. "You asked Marie to find you a man? Did she audition them naked?"

"Possibly."

He started to nod, and then his face fell. "I don't have anything to wear."

"Isn't that supposed to be my line?" At least that got a smile out of him. "I'll get you a suit."

"That doesn't sit right."

Okay, if we were ever going to get anywhere, one of us had to be up front. "Joe, last year I cleared two hundred thousand after tax, and I own this place outright." One advantage of working all hours and winning nearly every case I fought was that big fat bonus cheque. And when I'd put the deposit down, I'd planned to get a mortgage, but my father came round with a bottle of champagne, did his proud father speech, and then we both got drunk. Before he went home, he handed me a cheque for the rest, saying I might as well have his money before my mother spent it all. "And I was about to spend a thousand pounds hiring a perma-tanned escort for the evening. Please, let me buy you a suit."

"Am I ever going to win an argument with you?"

"Probably not."

He closed his eyes and shook his head, almost to himself. "None of this fancy made-to-measure business."

"I can live with that. Deal?" I held out my hand.

"Deal."

We shook, and a jolt of electricity ran up my arm as our palms touched. This new living situation promised to be frustrating as hell. Despite Joe's crack about taking advantage of me last night, he walked into the spare room without a backwards glance, leaving me a puddle of hormones and dirty thoughts.

And when he smiled at me in the hallway as we both went to leave, showing a row of perfect white teeth, those thoughts only promised to get filthier.

"Meet you back here at seven?" I suggested.

"I'll be here." He held an arm out. "Ready for Dane?"

I grabbed my bag and took my place at Joe's side, relishing the heaviness of his arm as it settled over my shoulders. "Ready."

"Then let's go."

CHAPTER 14

FRIDAY EVENING, AND I'd worked right up to six thirty and brought a few hours' work home with me so I didn't have to go back to the office until Monday. And when I walked through the gateway of Heron Court, my weekend got better because Joe was sitting on the low wall outside the front door, tapping away at his phone.

He put it back into his pocket when he saw me, and that wide smile made my whole year. He looked more relaxed today too, less rigid in the way he carried himself, and it took a couple of years off him. How old was he, anyway? I didn't even know. I'd guessed a little older than me, maybe thirty, but now I wasn't so sure.

"Good day?" he asked.

"Better now I'm home."

He picked up a Tesco bag and held the door open for me. "I thought I'd make mango chicken if you're okay with that?"

"I love chicken, but you don't have to cook."

"I like cooking, and it's been a while since I had a kitchen to do it in. I've missed it."

"In that case, the kitchen's yours."

Joe had already showered and changed into a pair of jeans at work, so I nipped into my bedroom to put on something more comfortable while he rummaged around in the kitchen. It was strange how settled I felt around him, right from the get-go. With the accountant, even when we stayed in to watch a movie in the evenings, I'd still put on make-up, fancy underwear, and a reasonably smart outfit, but with Joe, I pulled on yoga pants and a loose sweater before padding back to the kitchen barefoot.

I didn't feel like I needed to pretend anymore.

The cats were all in there watching him, no doubt hoping for chicken scraps and a bit of attention. I perched on one of the stools at the breakfast bar and Loki leapt onto my lap, demanding scritches while I took a sip from the glass of red Joe had poured for me.

"Did you find everything you needed?" I asked.

"Yeah. You've never used half of these utensils, have you?"

"I mostly eat takeout and ready meals."

"And the salmon in the fridge belongs to the cats?"

"How did you guess?" I slugged back half of the wine and took a deep breath. I didn't want to spoil the evening, but with so many questions about Joe's life still unanswered, I needed to get the unpleasantness over before I could relax. "Joe, we need to talk."

"I know."

"We're living together now, and I hardly know anything about you. Not your surname, your age, where you come from. I don't even have your phone number."

Joe said nothing as he opened up the oven and slid a tray full of chicken inside, then put rice on to boil. He moved slowly, deliberately, as if to delay answering, but finally he took a seat opposite me and filled his wine glass almost to the brim.

"My surname's Streeter, and I don't have a middle name. I'm twenty-eight."

"Same as me."

"Do you have your phone?"

I handed it over and watched him add his number before he pushed it back across the table.

"Those were the easy parts, huh?" I asked.

"Yeah." He took a long swallow of red. "So, how did I end up where I am today? It started when my mum died. I was twenty-three, Freya was fifteen, and a drunk driver ran Mum down on the road right outside our house."

My gasp echoed in the silence. "I'm so sorry."

"It wasn't your fault. The driver hit a wall afterwards, and he died too. He didn't even have insurance."

Shit. "So you had to look after your sister?"

"It wasn't that easy. I was in Iraq when it happened, and I couldn't get home for six weeks. Freya was coping better than me, or so I thought. Our next-door neighbours took her in. She'd been best friends with Hannah, their daughter, for as long as I can remember. She still is. They're sharing a flat together at uni. Their son, Craig, he was like my brother. We joined the army together, and he was with me in Iraq. He kept my shit together while Hannah and her parents looked after Freya."

Words seemed inadequate. I reached across the table and twined my fingers through Joe's, trying to offer him some comfort.

"I wanted to quit and take care of her myself, but you have to give a year's notice to leave the army, and by then she'd have been sixteen. The Colliers offered to become her legal guardians, and Freya told me that was the best arrangement for everyone."

"But it wasn't?"

"When I got back from Iraq, I was in the UK for a few months and I visited every weekend. She seemed okay. Quiet, but okay. I shipped out for another tour, eight months, but when I got back, she'd changed. Staying out late, going to parties. Nobody told me. I followed her one night and caught her snorting coke, and it only got worse. The Colliers couldn't cope anymore, and she ended up in A&E after an overdose. The doctors sent her to rehab, but it didn't help, and Hannah found her in the shower, bleeding everywhere."

He clutched his wrist as he spoke, and my stomach lurched. "She tried to kill herself?"

"Nearly succeeded. I used all my savings to send her to a private hospital, and she finally started to make some progress. I sold everything—my motorbike, my laptop, and the piece of land my grandfather left me."

My ears pricked up. Was this the property dispute he'd mentioned? "What happened with the land?"

He shook his head. "That part's off limits. Just know that I didn't do well out of the deal. But it paid for part of Freya's rehab, and I took out a loan to pay the rest. It was worth it to see her well again. And she's okay at the moment."

There was still a big jump between him being in the army and ending up homeless in London. "Is there more?"

"Yeah, there's more." He got up and walked to the window with his glass of wine, staring out into the darkness. "Me and Craig went back out to the Middle East again, for one last tour. Afghanistan that time. We were gonna set up a business together, doing carpentry.

His grandad taught us all that shit when we were teenagers—flooring, doors, staircases. Only Craig never came back."

"The Colliers must have been devastated," I whispered.

"They were. I saw them at the funeral, and they wouldn't even look at me. I was with him when he died, and I couldn't save him."

I heard the hitch in Joe's voice, and he raised his hand to wipe away the tears sparkling in his reflection in the kitchen window.

"Is that how you got the scar on your leg?"

He nodded. "A bullet."

All those hours I'd spent watching him, drawing him, never realising he had so much pain hidden away inside. It really put my problems with Dane into perspective.

"Have you spoken to anybody about this?"

"Just you."

Oh, hell. My stool made a horrible scraping sound as I pushed it back and went over to him. "Come here." I pulled him into a hug, and as he wrapped his arms around me, I felt his agony leaching out through the broken parts of him. It should have scared me, but all I wanted to do was put him back together again. And then after that, the selfish part of me wanted to keep him.

Dinner was a little awkward, and a little burnt too. The rice boiled dry and neither of us noticed until the smoke alarm went off, and when the chicken came out dry and crispy, I gave up and ordered a pizza.

"Sorry," Joe said. "This is what happens. Everything I touch at the moment turns to shit."

"We'll fix it."

He managed a lopsided smile. "I hate having you involved in all this."

"Too late now. You're stuck with me as your guidance counsellor."

"I'd rather you went back to being the hot girl who draws me once a week."

A charge jolted through my body at his words. He thought I was hot? Flipping heck! *Play it cool, Cate.* "I can draw you once a week if you like."

"Deal."

Holy hamburgers, did I just get my very own life drawing model? And did he mean naked drawing? If he did, I'd have to invest in waterproof knickers or things could get embarrassing. Thankfully, the door buzzer saved me from further discussions, and I rushed to let the pizza delivery guy inside. One deep pan with everything, and my mouth watered the instant I opened the door.

"So that's one large Supreme, a side order of potato wedges, and a pint of cookie-dough ice cream. And, er, someone left these chocolates on your doorstep. They're the posh kind."

"Thanks. You have a girlfriend?"

His brows knitted together. "Yes?"

"Why don't you take the chocolates for her? I've got plenty."

"Are you sure? They look expensive."

"I'm positive. Have a good evening."

I closed the door before he could argue any further, happy that I didn't have to try to squash yet another unwanted gift into my hall cupboard. Maybe I could sell the coffee machine on eBay? Or take it to a charity shop? Simply throwing it away seemed wasteful, but I didn't want it in my apartment.

But that could wait until tomorrow. Tonight, I had pizza, ice cream, and Joe, and out of those three, I knew which one was more delicious. The sexy guy walking towards me won the battle hands down.

CHAPTER 15

I MAY HAVE been slightly tipsy by the time I wobbled out of the lounge, stuffed with pizza and ice cream and wine, but after we'd watched a dodgy sci-fi movie with such bad CGI we laughed the whole way through, at least Joe was smiling again. And when I'd changed the batteries on my Rabbit and turned the TV up for ten minutes to cover the noise, so was I.

"Sleep well?" Joe asked the next morning.

"Mmm."

"Ready to hit the gym?"

"What?"

"Our deal, remember? The personal training part? I made smoothies."

Too late, I noticed he was wearing his shorts and one of those little vests that showed off his chest muscles. "Could we start tomorrow?"

"What kind of trainer would I be if I let you skip out on the first session?"

"My kind of trainer?"

He folded his arms and stared at me. "Go and get changed."

"Yes, sir. Can I have coffee first?"

"There's something in a Starbucks cup sitting outside your front door."

"Perhaps I'll pass on the coffee."

"Good plan."

The gym was dark when we arrived, and I flicked on the lights and cranked up the air conditioner. For a private gym, the place was surprisingly well equipped, with a good range of cardio and weight machines, plus mats and free weights in one corner.

"What do you usually do?" Joe asked.

"I've barely been to the gym in years, but I used to walk on the treadmill for a bit then cycle until my legs stopped working."

"Weights?"

I quickly shook my head. "I don't know where to start with those. Won't I end up all muscly?"

"Not unless you're into steroids. Adding a few light weights into your routine will help you to tone up."

"So, where do I start?"

"On the treadmill, but you're jogging, not walking."

Why had I ever thought this arrangement was a good idea? My thighs jiggled as Joe turned the speed up faster, and I cringed as I caught sight of my decidedly unattractive reflection in the mirror. *Please, Joe, don't look down.*

I tried to talk to him so he'd keep his attention on my face, but I was soon puffing away, and it was all I could do to keep going until the timer hit five minutes and Joe slowed the sodding machine down.

"And you call me a ball-buster?" I choked out.

The bastard just smiled. "You don't have any balls to bust."

"Slave driver."

"Time to get on the rowing machine."

"Aren't you going to do anything?"

"I'll hop on the treadmill once you get going."

Ten minutes later, my arms barely had the strength to pick up my water bottle, while Joe had run two miles without even breaking a sweat.

"What now?" I asked. "Breakfast?"

"Close. Bike."

"Please, spare me, I—"

Both our heads turned as the door opened, and Dane walked in, channelling the eighties in green neon sweatbands and the skimpy shorts of a long-distance runner.

"Change of plans," Joe murmured into my ear. "Let's switch to weights."

"But I don't know what I'm doing."

"Not a problem."

Oh, it was a problem all right. As Joe demonstrated every move by wrapping his body around mine and lifting the weights with me, my nipples stood to attention and *that* spot between my thighs throbbed. The girl looking back at us from the mirror had flushed cheeks and a ridiculous smile on her face, and I prayed my yoga pants wouldn't end up with a damp patch. I'd turned into a hot mess of hormones and lust and we were both still fully clothed. Yes, I was definitely in trouble.

"Have you noticed Dane?" Joe whispered.

I made an effort to focus. "He looks...pissed. Really pissed."

Joe slid his hand down a little lower, so it rested right on my bottom, and grinned. "Good. Now we can have breakfast."

***

It was almost disappointing when Dane didn't turn up in the gym the next morning, partly because I'd enjoyed annoying him but mostly because it meant Joe kept his hands off me. Still, I felt better after a workout even if I hated to admit it.

"Do you train people all day?" I asked Joe.

"Not like this. The place I work is more of a boxing gym, and most of my clients are men."

"You box? Isn't that dangerous?"

"Not competitively, not anymore. I do more sparring than anything, and I always wear pads now."

"You used to box competitively?"

"I was on the army boxing team for a couple of years."

All these things I didn't know about him, and I craved the details. Joe fascinated me, this man who'd lost so much and then given up everything he had left to help his sister. Fascinated me and turned me the hell on.

"I've got an evening shift today," he said after we'd both showered. "Five until midnight."

"Does that mean you've got time to get a suit first?"

"My day is yours."

Now, Joe naked may have made my insides flip, but when he put on a tailored suit, I had to remind myself to keep breathing. We'd ended in Moss Bros. I'd wanted Saville Row and Joe tried to go to Next, so we'd compromised at a price point in the middle. And as an added bonus, I guess since I'd seen it all already, he didn't seem too worried about keeping the curtain in the changing room pulled right across, and I got a good eyeful of him in his underwear. This man was going to be the death of me.

"What do you think of this one?"

Charcoal grey, slim fit. My eyes may have been a tad glazed by then. "It's a bit tight across the shoulders."

Those muscles. Mmmm.

"You preferred the light grey one?"

"I'll see what else there is." Not that the light grey suit didn't look good, more because I could have watched Joe model suits all day.

And he was a good sport about it. He must have put on twenty different ones by the time we settled on a French-blue two-piece that matched his eyes, plus a white shirt, grey tie, and pair of Oxfords to go with it. I wanted to buy him a new coat too, but he shook his head.

"Enough, Catie."

"Okay. I suppose I still need to get a dress to match. But you don't need to come," I added hastily.

"What, and pass up the chance to see you parading round in fancy-ass clothes after what you just put me through? I don't think so. Where to?"

"Selfridges."

"Your favourite shop?"

"Not my favourite, exactly, but the one I hate least. Nothing ever fits. But if I go to Selfridges, everything's under one roof, which is somehow less depressing, and there's a bar for when it all gets too much."

"I thought women loved shopping?"

"Not this one. I buy almost everything online."

Joe picked the suit up and put an arm around my shoulders. "What can I do to make it easier?"

Just don't move that arm. "Uh, maybe just give your opinion on what looks least horrible?"

"You mean the most beautiful."

This man was too damn sweet.

It turned out shopping with Joe was a whole different experience to shopping on my own, mainly because three assistants hovered around us permanently in case he might possibly need a hand with anything. Each time he pointed them in my direction they sighed and huffed a little, but I did end up with a pile of dresses to try on while they settled Joe onto a sofa outside the fitting room with a complimentary glass of wine and a lot of batting of eyelashes.

Lacking Joe's confidence or perfect physique, I kept the curtain firmly closed as I zipped myself into one dress after another. Most went on the "no" pile right away, but a few looked all right enough for me to show him.

"None of them do you justice," he said when I walked out in the fourth outfit.

"There's only one left."

"The grey one?"

"How do you know?"

"It was my favourite when they brought it in."

And it might have been mine too if I could get the damn thing done up. "I can't reach the zipper. Is one of those girls still around?"

"The last one deserted me when I turned down her dinner invite. Want me to help?"

"Uh..." I'd taken my bra off because it was a halter-neck, but if I held on tight to the front... "Okay."

His breath on the back of my neck made my insides churn like a washing machine as he slowly zipped the dress up, all the way from my bottom to my shoulder blades. When he'd finished, he smoothed the silk over my hips and took a step back.

"That's the dress."

He was right. I twirled in front of the mirror, and the bodice did awesome things to my cleavage while the flared skirt hid the bottom of my stomach. Not only that, the colour matched the tie we'd bought Joe earlier perfectly.

"I'll buy it."

"You want me to unfasten you?"

"Please."

Warm fingertips brushed my skin as he inched the zipper downwards, pausing for a moment to sweep my hair out of the way. My self-control was hanging by a thread by the time he'd finished, and every limb itched to push him back against the wall and press my lips against his. He'd turned me into some wanton lunatic actually contemplating doing the deed in a public changing room, and all with a few feathery touches.

Just as I was about to self-combust, he stepped back. "You still want to stop by the bar?"

I didn't just need a flute of champagne, I needed a bottle, plus the contents of the ice bucket dumped over my head.

"A glass of bubbly would be good, yes."

"I'll get a table and meet you down there."

CHAPTER 16

BY SUNDAY EVENING, Marie's patience had run out. My phone rang as Joe and I were in a taxi heading back to Heron Court, squashed in beside my dress and his suit, together with the sparkly necklace I'd impulse bought on the way out of Selfridges in an attempt to provide a further distraction from my waistline.

"Come on, spill," she said. "It's been three days since you ran out of art class and not even a phone call? Did you find him?"

"I did."

Her squeal made Joe look across, and I held the phone away from my ear for a second.

"And? What happened?"

"Uh, not very much."

"Seriously? A tattooed sex god bought you a gift, you sprinted after him in the pouring rain, and nothing happened? I don't believe it."

"Now isn't a great time to talk."

She put two and two together and came up with seven thousand and sixty-nine. "OMG! He's with you! Am I right? Is he?"

"Yes."

"Okay, okay, I'm gone. But I want to hear all about it on Thursday. Every detail. Don't I always tell you everything?"

"Yes, but I don't want to hear it."

"Eve-ry-thing."

She hung up and I stared at the phone, rolling my eyes because Marie had such a one-track mind. Ninety percent of her thoughts revolved around sex, which was probably why she was so good at her job working as a buyer for a well-known chain of adult stores.

"What's up?" Joe asked. "Was that Marie?"

"Yes."

"I thought I recognised the screech."

"She wants to know what's happening with us. She was there when I came after you last week, and I left her with all my art stuff."

"What will you tell her?"

"Not the truth, that's for sure. The truth is crazy. How would I explain I invited you to move in after two dinners and one conversation?"

"I don't know. I still don't understand it myself."

"Besides, it's not my secret to tell."

He reached across and twined his fingers through mine. "Thank you."

I closed my eyes as he stroked his thumb across my knuckles. "But I'll have to tell her something, and she worked out we were together this afternoon. How about I say we met up for a drink, and we're going out for dinner next week? That'll buy us time."

He brought my hand to his lips and kissed the back of it. "Looks like I'm taking you out for dinner again."

I couldn't help smiling. "Looks like you are."

***

Dane must have known Joe was staying with me, not

least because we put on a show for him every time we walked along the hallway. Those were my favourite parts of the day. A soft kiss on my hair, a hand resting on my waist, Joe's fingers running through my hair. And yes, Joe's buttocks were every bit as firm as they looked. But the gifts kept coming, and although Battersea Dogs & Cats Home was very grateful for the box of goodies I couriered over to them, I was reaching the end of my tether.

"Do you think it'll ever stop?" I asked Joe as we got ready to leave on Thursday morning.

"Hopefully when he realises I'm not leaving."

"It's like he still reckons he's got a chance. I don't understand."

"He's sprung in the head. There's nothing rational about it."

"At least I feel safe at home now. He'd started to really scare me, especially when I got back late."

Joe tucked me under his arm as he unlocked the front door. I'd given him his own key now, so I didn't have to worry about rushing home from work in the evenings to let him in. He'd repaid me by making dinner every night, and when I'd stepped on the scales this morning, I'd lost three pounds with the exercise and healthier eating. Another reason to smile as we walked towards the lift.

"Call me when you're ready to leave class tonight. I'll be hanging around outside where Marie can't see me. You say she always goes right?"

"Yes, towards the Tube station."

Joe nibbled my earlobe as the elevator doors closed, and usually he'd have let me go at that point, with the need to entertain Dane over until the evening. But today he kept me plastered against his chest, and I rested my chin against his shoulder until the chime signalled we'd reached the ground floor. Even then he didn't release my hand, not until we went our separate ways at the Tube station.

"See you later, Catie. Call me, remember."

"I won't forget."

***

My hand stayed warm from Joe's touch all day, right up until the moment it found its way back into his after art class in the evening. Even Mr. Berkeley's incessant moaning about the firm's team-building weekend clashing with his favourite golf tournament hadn't put a dent in my mood, and true to his word, Joe met me outside and even carried my stuff as we walked back home.

"Good class?"

"We had to draw fruit."

I'd attempted a persimmon paired with half a kiwi, while Marie, predictably, had picked out two plums and a banana.

"You'd rather have painted meat and two veg?"

I shoved him away, laughing. "Stop it. You're as bad as Marie. Did I tell you she wants me to go to an underwear exhibition at the V&A with her?"

"Good grief." He rolled his eyes. "Did you get interrogated?"

"I got off lightly. She spent most of the evening sexting with Andy, and at one point a threesome was mentioned. She left pretty sharpish."

It was Joe's turn to laugh. "I'm glad it was you who

came after me that night rather than her. Otherwise, I'd probably be tied down in a dungeon right now while she dripped candle wax on my backside and questioned me about my sexual preferences."

"I can't even..." I put my hand over his mouth to stop him from expanding on that hideous vision. "Speaking of interrogations, are you ready for Saturday?"

"Meeting your parents? I don't think any guy ever is."

"I'm so sorry. There's still time to back out."

"And have you go with another man? Not likely."

"My mother won't like you, but it's nothing personal. She judges everyone by which clubs they're a member of, how much money they have, and what labels they're wearing. She forgets that she was working as an air stewardess on Concorde when she met my father."

"I'll try to keep out of her way."

"She'll be on the sauce straight away, and she'll forget your name by eight thirty." Probably mine too if she got out the good stuff. Hendricks with cucumber, never with lime, or a dry martini with two olives. The glass had damn well better be chilled, or the bartender's next job would be mixing cocktails at a beach bar in Benidorm.

"That's one positive. What about your dad?"

"He's not so superficial as Mum, but he does have a tendency to get a little overprotective. And he's also a lawyer. Well, a barrister."

"So I'm in for a grilling, then?"

"You might want to wear asbestos underwear."

And I'd need to stand ready with the fire

extinguisher.

***

Damn, Joe scrubbed up well. He'd got his hair cut and spiked it up with gel, and with his freshly shaved cheeks, his strong jaw looked all the more lickable. And I still couldn't get my damn dress done up.

"Can you help me with the zip again?"

"Sure."

How did he look so unruffled? I'd been to a hundred of these events over the years and I wanted to throw up from the nerves, and Joe was relaxing on the sofa, watching a program on house renovations. Maybe it was because I knew what to expect. Barbs from my mother about my appearance. Being stared at like an exhibit. Whispers of, "Has Catherine put on weight? She's not expecting, is she?"

Well, not unless it was the immaculate bloody conception.

And when Joe ran his fingers up my back along with the zip, I felt even more unsettled than normal.

I'd visited the hairdresser too, so at least my hair looked okay, but as usual I'd had two goes at my make-up and scrubbed it all off again. Some girls were designed to wear eyeliner and strong lipstick, but I wasn't one of them. In the end, I went with a swipe of mascara and dark pink lip gloss, so at least Mother couldn't complain I'd made no effort at all.

At half past six, Joe peered out the window. "Cab's here."

Wonderful. The hour of doom had arrived.

I draped a pashmina over my shoulders, and Joe

put his arm around my waist.

"You look beautiful."

"You don't need to start with the bullshit until we get to the party."

He tilted my chin towards him and held my eyes. "You look beautiful."

His gaze bored into me, and I looked away first. Why was the bad stuff always easier to believe?

"Shall we get going?"

I asked the driver to circle the block a couple of times when we arrived, just to let a few more guests in before us and hopefully distract Mother. I might have been tempted to let him drive round and round all night if Joe hadn't reminded me of the time.

"It's almost seven thirty, and the sooner we go in, the sooner we can leave."

"You're right. Of course you're right."

A waiter took my wrap at the door, and I leaned into Joe for support as we walked into my parents' palatial living room. They could have fitted a whole orchestra in there, but Mother had settled for a string quartet playing in one corner.

I'd chugged back half a glass of champagne before she spotted us, and when she called my name, I felt Joe stiffen beside me too. Then she headed in our direction, eyes locked on Joe as she assessed the newcomer.

"Darling, who's this?"

"Joe."

"That boy you said you'd been dating?"

"Yes, this is him."

Mother looked him up and down, but her face gave nothing away as she leaned forward and offered him a cheek to kiss. He looked confused for a second before he touched his lips to her slightly orange skin. She'd developed an obsession with fake tan after her cosmetic surgeon told her to keep out of the sun to avoid more wrinkles.

"And what do you do, Moe?"

"It's Joe, Mum."

She stared at him expectantly, holding out one hand for a passing waiter to place a drink into.

"I work in a gym."

"At head office?"

"No, I train people."

"Oh. Like a tennis instructor?" Mother understood tennis instructors. The ladies at her health club passed them around like candy.

"No, boxing."

There was a sharp intake of breath. "A word in private, Catherine."

I looked back helplessly at Joe as Mother dug her talons into my arm and dragged me into the third reception room, then closed the door.

"Honestly, Catherine. A boxing instructor?"

"I like him."

"I still don't understand why you're not with Bruce anymore."

"Because Bruce cared more about who Daddy was than me. Did you know he used to introduce me to his acquaintances as Roderick Jenkins' daughter rather than Cate?"

"I should hope so too. Cate's such a common name."

As usual, she'd completely missed my point. "I really like Joe, Mum."

"A gym instructor will never be able to support

you."

"He doesn't have to. I make my own money, just like Daddy insisted I had to."

"Your father didn't expect you to work for the rest of your life. It's high time you got married and started a family, but you need to find a suitable husband first. You're twenty-seven now, Catherine, and your biological clock is ticking."

"I'm twenty-eight."

"Are you? I must have missed a year." That coming from the woman who'd celebrated her thirty-ninth birthday eleven times. "The situation is worse than I thought. I really must call Verity Barrington-Foster."

"Don't you dare! I'm with Joe, and I don't want anybody else."

"Don't you speak to me that way, young lady."

"Then have some respect for my choices."

"I will when you start making the right ones." She took a step back and squinted. "Have you put on weight again?"

That was it. I'd had enough of Mother and her harsh comments for one night. I stormed out, not caring that the door slammed behind me, and hurried back to the sanctuary of the living room and Joe.

Only to find him deep in conversation with my father. *Please, don't let him be mean as well.*

"Everything okay, pumpkin?" he asked.

My cheeks heated at the use of my old childhood nickname. "No."

Joe wrapped an arm around my waist and I leaned into him. Before I could stop myself, I liberated his wine from his hand and swallowed the entire glassful.

"You've spoken to your mother, then?" my father

asked.

"Yes."

"I've just been speaking to your young man."

"Please, don't you start as well."

"I was just going to say how glad I am that you've found someone who genuinely cares for you. Not like that bloody accountant."

"Really?"

"And an army man as well. Did his bit for our country, and we should all be grateful."

"I am."

"His grandfather was a lawyer too. Patents."

He was? "Uh, yes."

Daddy patted me on the stomach. "So that blood'll keep running through the family when you settle down. And isn't it lucky Joe here enjoys gardening? I'll have somebody to keep me company in the potting shed when your mother's on the warpath."

I caught a glimpse of Joe out of the corner of my eye, and he was trying to keep a straight face.

"I'm not sure he'll have time for that."

"Nonsense. We don't see enough of you as it is. Oh, Jack Prosser's arrived, and I need to speak to him about next week's golf tournament." Daddy patted Joe on the back. "Take care of my daughter, Mr. Streeter."

"You've got my word on that, sir."

"Happy birthday, Daddy."

"It's just another Saturday, pumpkin."

CHAPTER 17

"PLEASE, DON'T MAKE me go to the gym this morning. My feet hurt and my head hurts more," I begged Joe.

Following Daddy's lead last night, I'd hit the red and got more than a little bit drunk while Mother gave me dirty looks from across the room. Or maybe they were aimed at Joe. I'd been too sozzled to focus properly. Ever the hero, my fake boyfriend had scooped me up at the end of the night and carried me to the taxi while my parents looked on.

"I know your mother's not impressed, but that young man seems far better than the last one," Daddy had told me as Mother tutted behind him.

And now Joe passed me a glass of orange juice and a packet of paracetamol and pointed at a stool. "Lucky for you, the slave driver is feeling generous. I'm cooking you breakfast instead."

"Did I tell you what a fantastically amazing boyfriend you make? What did you say to my father, anyway? You really convinced him that you care about me."

"I didn't say anything that wasn't true. How about you and your mother? You shot out of that room looking like you wanted to murder someone."

"Oh, just the usual. I have terrible choice in men,

and I look like I've put on a few pounds."

Joe abandoned the eggs he was beating into submission and wrapped me up in his arms. "Don't let her put you down. You're the smartest woman I've ever met, and you're beautiful inside and out."

"That's difficult to believe when I've been told something different my whole life."

"You're not even halfway through, so there's plenty of time to change that, starting now."

"You're too sweet, Joe."

He kissed my hair then went back to his mixing bowl. "How do you like your eggs in the morning?"

"Is this the bit where I'm supposed to say 'unfertilised'?"

"Shit. That wasn't supposed to be the worst chat-up line of all time, honest."

"No, that would be the man in a bar who told me I was like a termite because I was going to get a mouthful of wood tonight."

"A man actually said that to you?"

"I'm not sure I'd class him as a man. Come on, what's the worst line a girl's used on you?"

"Hmm, the weirdest one was a girl who said she wanted to paint me green and spank me like a disobedient avocado."

"She what? You made that up."

"Nope. Deadly serious, I swear. And at least you're smiling now."

I couldn't help it, not with Joe in my kitchen.

"And you didn't answer my question—how do you like your eggs? Fried? Scrambled? Poached?"

Fertilised.

"Whatever you're having is fine."

"Scrambled, then. What are you doing for the rest of the day? Do you have more work?"

"No, I got it all done yesterday. Today, I'm going to paint. It's the only thing that gets rid of the stress after a run-in with Mother."

Joe rolled an orange in my direction. "I can offer fruit, or my services as a model."

"You were serious about that?"

"We had a deal, and lying on your couch for an hour or two isn't exactly a hardship."

If he was offering, I couldn't turn him down. Drawing from a live model gave a depth a photograph could never achieve, plus, you know, muscles.

"In that case, thank you."

***

An hour later, I spread the fruits of last month's labours out on the dining table. Five poses, five pictures of Joe.

"Why did you only draw my face in the last session?" he asked.

"It's my favourite part of you to look at, but your eyes were so sad that day."

"Because I didn't think I'd see you again."

And if I'd looked into a mirror, my eyes would have been a reflection of his. How things had changed in just a few short weeks. We both smiled more and that horrible sense of despair I'd felt had evaporated.

Joe glanced over at the couch. "So, where do you want me, boss?"

I pointed at my unfinished drawing from week four. "Could you lie like that again? That way I can fill in the detail."

He nodded. "Everything off?"

Much as I wanted to say yes, I didn't want to make him feel awkward. Leching over a hot man in a controlled, professional environment was one thing, but in the comfort of my own home? Wouldn't that be considered odd?

"No need. As long as I can see your chest and legs." Which basically meant, "Keep your boxer briefs on."

After one quick glance at his impressive bulge, I forced my eyes upwards and concentrated on shading the muscles in his arms. An hour passed as my drawing came to life, then two, and Joe's soft, rhythmical breathing told me he'd fallen asleep. I stifled a giggle as I threw a cushion at him.

"Hey! No sleeping on the job."

His eyes flew open as he grabbed at the cushion. "What? What happened?"

"You fell asleep."

"Shit. Sorry."

"It doesn't matter. Can you turn a little to your left? Or do you want to finish for the day?"

He shifted slightly. "Like this?"

"Perfect."

"I'll try not to fall asleep again."

"It doesn't matter. I'm not surprised that you drop off if you keep staring at the ceiling. Why don't you ever look at me? You rarely did in class either."

"I couldn't, not with everybody else around."

"I suppose Delores might have thought it odd if you paid one student extra attention."

"Yeah, something like that."

"But you can look at me today now we're on our

own, can't you?"

"I guess I can."

And boy, did he. The looks he gave me were smouldering, and I grabbed a new sketchbook and began drawing his face again instead, trying not to squirm too much on my chair as my knickers grew wetter and wetter.

"Does this work for you, Catie?" His voice was different, huskier.

I forced a laugh. "Perfect. See, that's not so hard, is it?"

"Oh, it's very hard."

"Why?"

His eyes flicked downwards, and I realised the bulge in his pants had grown considerably since the start of the session. Cheese and rice, was the man hiding a salami in there?

"Now you see why I never looked at you in class? Because everyone would have known what was going through my mind."

And at the moment, *my* mind was screaming, "WHAT THE HELL?"

"I-I-I don't get it."

"Some men like curvy girls, and I'm one of them. You think I'm a gentleman, but if you knew what I was thinking right now, you'd change that opinion pretty fucking fast."

"Tell me." It came out as a croak.

He sighed and shifted so he wasn't looking at me anymore, and when he reached a hand down to adjust himself, I almost came on the spot.

"Right now, I'm thinking how close you came to being fucked in a changing room in Selfridges last week. How I wanted to bend you over that padded bench, push your knickers to one side, and watch myself slide in and out of you while those gorgeous tits bounced in the mirror."

Holy hell, I could barely breathe. "But you left."

"I went to the bar via the men's room because my cock was so hard it hurt."

As I pictured him leaning against the wall of a bathroom stall, jeans unzipped, belt hanging loose as his hand disappeared into his underwear, my insides clenched with the first flutters of an orgasm. *And he hadn't even touched me.*

"But you've never done so much as kiss me properly."

"Still waiting for you to come to your senses and realise your mother's right in one respect at least."

Dammit, if we did this dance much longer, I was going to explode. His head was still turned away as I crossed the room on shaky legs and dropped to my knees at his side.

"Joe, look at me."

He did, a sheepish smile on his face, and I couldn't hold back any longer, not with the air practically crackling between us. I'd never made the first move before, not once, but when my lips met his, it was as if I'd pressed the nuclear button. One touch and he'd pinned me under him. I didn't realise a man could move so fast.

His weight and that delicious hardness pressed into me as our tongues clashed, and with the absence of clothing, I raked my fingernails down his back. He fisted his hands in my hair as I rubbed against him, desperate for some relief from the tension building inside me.

"Please, Joe." Oh good grief, I'd freaking whimpered.

"What do you want me to do, Catie?"

Uh, carry on nibbling my earlobe like he did right then? No, more. "Touch me. Make me come."

A hand inched downwards, over the stomach I'd always hated so much, and settled over the magic spot.

"Fuck, Catie. These yoga pants are damp."

Oh, someone kill me now. "I hate them."

"I don't. I love them. They show every luscious curve, and I've dreamed of doing this." He flipped us so I was on top, reached both hands behind me, and then tore the pants open along the seam. "Better."

Please, say I'd worn the good panties this morning. I screwed my eyes shut, thinking... Black-and-pink lace, and by some miracle, a bra that matched. Thank goodness.

And then Joe's thumb was on me, circling oh-so-slowly as he slipped one long finger inside. He rolled us again, and I dropped my head back and bit my lip hard enough to draw blood as he dipped down to whisper his filthy thoughts.

"You're tight, Catie. You're gonna fit my cock like a fucking glove. My Catie. Because once I've come inside you, that's it. No other man is getting near you."

"I don't want any other man. Please..."

He added a second finger, stroking *that* spot deep inside until I panted into his mouth. Then his thumb joined in again, lifting me higher, higher.

"Are you gonna scream my name when you come, beautiful?"

"Yes," I gasped. "Just, please..."

He chuckled maddeningly, and I pressed against him, trying to get him to hurry up.

"Good things come to those who wait." He kissed me again, smiling against my lips, and I ran my fingers through that dirty-blond hair I found so sexy. Bedroom hair, even if we were still on the couch.

"But I don't want to—"

He pressed with his thumb and my orgasm tore through me, and yes, I screamed his name, loud enough for Dane to hear and probably most of north London as well.

"That was...just...just..."

"The beginning," Joe finished for me.

My legs were still shaking as he carried me through to my bedroom—no, our bedroom, because he wouldn't be sleeping in the spare room again after this. With every step, that magnificent cock pressed against me, and although I'd always been a once-a-night girl, I could feel another orgasm building already.

"Tell me you've got condoms," he said as he laid me on the bed.

"Uh..." Shit! I rolled over to the nightstand and yanked the drawer open. Please say the accountant had done one useful thing during his tenure in my bedroom. I rummaged around as Joe leaned over and plucked my Rampant Rabbit out of its case.

"Put that down!" And let me die quietly of embarrassment.

But he didn't. No, he pulled his boxers down so his own cock sprang free and held them side by side, comparing. And that cocky smirk he wore was deserved in every way.

"Seeing as I've got an inch on this, I think you can

throw it away."

I snatched it from his hand and hurled it out the door. "Gone. And I found this." I held up my prize, a Durex Ultra Thin I'd found lurking behind my phone charger, still two months inside the expiration date, thank goodness.

"Only one? Guess we'll be going shopping later." He peeled my sweater over my head. "But first I want to see those delicious tits."

He'd lost his pants, and once he'd made short work of the rest of my clothes, there was nothing between us as he licked and sucked his way down my body, leaving a trail of fire as he grazed his lips over my skin. And when he paused between my legs and added his tongue to his fingers, I arched up off the bed and screamed his name again.

As I floated back to earth, I heard the rip of foil, and when I opened my eyes, that solid cock was hovering by my entrance, ready to lift me right back up again.

"Okay?" he whispered.

"Always, with you."

He slid slowly inside, and I'd never been stretched like that before. He had the Rabbit beaten on girth too. We both sighed as he settled himself to the root and stilled for a moment.

"For the record, Miss Jenkins, I've been crazy about you since the first night we met."

"I was a mess."

"You were beautiful. Still are, and always will be."

I realised then that everything I'd done with the viscount and the accountant was just a poor imitation. Joe didn't have sex. He made love, and I could feel it seeping from every pore as he moved against me. For the first time ever, he made me feel sexy, desired. And his.

This time, the orgasm built in a slow wave, and when I surfed over the crest, it was more intense than anything I'd ever experienced. Joe followed me, filling me with his heat as he whispered my name against my lips.

Was it too soon for the "L" word? Because I knew right then I'd fallen in it.

Even after we both came, he didn't stop. He hovered over me, peppering my face and neck with soft kisses as we both tried to get our breath back.

"I didn't even know it could be like that," I murmured.

"Only with you, Catie. Only with you." He propped himself up on one elbow, looking down at the mess of tangled sheets and the sweat glistening on our bodies. "I feel like you should paint this moment for posterity."

"I've got several shades of green. I reckon I could do an avocado."

He broke into a wide grin. "You want to spank me, madam?"

I shrugged, matching his smile with one of my own. "Would you enjoy it?"

What on earth had come over me?

"Eh, I'll try anything once."

CHAPTER 18

I DID GET my eggs unfertilised the next morning, but only because Joe and I walked to the convenience store on the corner last night and stocked up on supplies. Milk, orange juice, five boxes of condoms, a lasagne, wine, and a bottle of chocolate sauce. I didn't know what Joe planned to do with the chocolate sauce, but he had a gleam in his eye when he put it into the basket.

By 7 a.m., we'd already made a dent in the condom supply, and Joe was muttering about buying them in bulk.

"I'm going to be late for work," I said.

I hopped around the kitchen, straightening my new pair of tights while Joe sorted out the coffee. The first pair I'd put on had fallen victim to Joe's fingernails, when he'd let me know just how much he liked my backside in a pencil skirt. I'd certainly never look at the kitchen island in the same way again, and the feel of the cold marble against my breasts and cheek as he bent me over it had done little to cool down my overheated libido.

"What do you still have left to do?"

"Brush my teeth. Feed the cats. Check the doorstep for Dane's offerings."

"I'll sort out the cats and Dane's shit. You only need to brush your teeth."

I gave him a quick peck on the lips as I ran past to the bathroom. "My hero."

It scared me how fast I'd settled into this life with Joe. How comfortable it felt, as if I'd known him for years instead of weeks. The pessimist in me whispered how it was too good to be true, that as soon as I relaxed, the rug would be pulled out from under my feet. But that morning as I walked along the hallway to the lift, I shoved all those thoughts to the side. Joe would never hurt me. Would he?

"Did I tell you how beautiful you look this morning?" He guided me into the elevator, and the moment the doors closed he pushed me against the wall for a searing kiss. The poor delivery man waiting at the bottom when they opened again got a right eyeful. Oops.

Joe had worn jeans this morning, and as we walked in the direction of the Tube station, I slipped my hand into his back pocket and squeezed.

"You've got no idea how long I've wanted to do that."

"If I did the things I've been wanting to do out here on the street, we'd both get arrested."

"What time are you back this evening?"

"My shift finishes at five."

***

I practically floated into work that morning, and even Mr. Berkeley's announcement that this year's senior staff team-building week would culminate in a two-day mock survival exercise in the Lake District barely dampened my spirits.

"Sleeping outside in October? Is he mad?" I whispered to Reggie.

"The senior partners are staying in a five-star golf resort. His PA said."

So it'd just be the managers and junior partners roughing it in the woods? Why didn't that surprise me?

And Mr. Berkeley wasn't done yet. "To make things more interesting this year, we thought everyone could bring their partners as well. You know, be more sociable and all that."

"That's because the firm got slammed in a recruitment survey about work/life balance last week," Reggie told me. "Guess you guys get to bring life to work with you now."

The kitchen was alive with the sound of complaints when I shuffled through to get my second espresso of the day. My work/life balance may have been abysmal, but my sex/sleep balance also needed some thinking through before I keeled over completely.

As usual, Sonia's voice was the loudest. "My new boyfriend runs an art gallery. I'm sure he won't want to sleep in a tent overnight."

"What happened to the investment guy from downstairs?" Sally asked.

"Yeah, that didn't work out. Turned out he was a vegan and his shoes were made from pleather."

Linda picked up her cappuccino and hovered in front of the coffee machine, blocking my way. "I don't know which boyfriend to bring."

"What are the choices?" Sally asked.

"The banker's a no because he won't want to get his fingernails dirty. That leaves the bike courier with calves sculpted by Michelangelo himself, or the biology undergrad from Clapham."

"An undergrad? Isn't he a bit young?"

"He's twenty-one, but he puts the stud in student."

And the D in STD, I bet. "Excuse me, can I get to the coffee machine?"

"Sure. At least you won't have a problem, Cate."

"Sorry?"

"Well, being single."

Would Joe come? Yeah, Joe would come. "I'm not single."

Six heads swivelled in my direction, like a herd of meerkats.

"Reeeeeally? Do tell," Sonia said.

I couldn't help smiling. "I think I'll keep the details to myself for now."

By the time I got back to my desk, the rumours were already circulating.

"Is it true you're seeing Bruce again?" Reggie asked. "Why am I always the last to know?"

"No! Where on earth did you hear that?"

He waved his phone at me. "The interns have a group on WhatsApp. No, wait... You're dating the UPS guy?"

"What UPS guy?"

"Then who?"

"It's a new thing. I don't want it being talked about all over the office."

Reggie kicked the door shut and perched on the edge of my desk. "My lips are sealed."

"Fine. His name's Joe and he works in a gym."

"That's it? Nothing juicy."

Juicy? Only the way I'd sucked Joe's... "Nope. Just not that interesting."

He shook his head and sighed in mock annoyance. "I suppose you're gonna give me some work to do on this fine Monday morning?"

"The thought had crossed my mind."

***

I shot out of the door at six thirty, right after Mr. Berkeley left for his squash game. Joe had texted me a picture of an avocado at five thirty and a cucumber at six, and as I dashed down the steps to the Tube station, a photo of my bed popped up on the screen. I almost tripped over in my hurry to get on the train, and a smartly dressed man gave me a dirty look as my hand landed dangerously near to his crotch.

"Sorry."

With no signal in the tunnel, I couldn't message back until I got back up to the street, but when I did, I sent two fried eggs. Joe's reply of the bottle of chocolate sauce didn't arrive until the elevator dinged for the third floor, and I was so busy laughing I didn't notice Dane until I walked right into him.

"Oof."

"Cate."

He didn't look happy as he stood blocking the corridor.

"Can I get past, please?"

"Still whoring around with that man you picked up off the street?"

"*What?* How *dare* you?"

"The gifts weren't enough? The dinner invitations? The interest in your hobbies? I turn my back for two minutes and you bring a homeless man round to live in your flat."

What business was it of his? And more to the point... "How do you know that?"

"Please, Cate, I'm not dumb. He turned up late one evening with a rucksack and a sleeping bag. What can he possibly offer you that I can't?"

Sanity?

"Just get out of my way."

"He might be in there cooking you dinner, but he'll never be able to take you out to a fancy restaurant. And what will your parents think? Your friends?"

For once I was glad to have brought work home with me, because when I swung my bag of files up into Dane's genitals, he doubled over with a satisfying groan. Heart pounding, I shoved past him and fumbled my key in the lock, then burst into tears the moment I got the door shut behind me.

"Cate? Catie?"

Joe reached me almost instantly, cradling me in his arms as I sobbed. "Dane," I choked out. "He said some really nasty things."

"I'll kill him. I swear, I'll kill the bastard."

Joe moved towards the door, but I grabbed his hand. "Please don't hurt him. You'll only get in trouble, and besides, he left."

I'd heard the lift doors close as I struggled with my key.

"Come and sit down."

Joe carried me through to the lounge and settled me onto the couch where only a day ago we'd been so blissfully happy.

"What did Dane say?"

I ran through the conversation, and when I got to

the bit about my family and friends finding out about Joe's origins, I started shaking. "Do you think he'll tell them?"

"I don't know, sweetheart. The guy's whacked." Joe's voice went quiet. "What would happen if he did?"

I didn't have to be a genius to understand Joe's real question—was I ashamed of him?

Of course not.

So, what would happen? My mother hated him already, so no difference there. My father... Well, he'd be shocked, but like he'd said at the party, Joe cared about me. And now I realised just how much.

Marie would think the situation was hilarious, so that left work. I'd be the main topic of gossip, no doubt about that, but today had already shown me I would be anyway, whether the story was true or not. Ultimately, the only thing that mattered was my feelings for Joe, and those were already clear to me.

"It would highlight, once again, what an arsehole Dane is."

"That's it?"

I twisted around and pressed my lips to his, and that kiss turned into something entirely more passionate.

"That's it."

"I feel like I should send Delores a present for bringing you to me," Joe said.

"Same. A fruit basket?"

We both laughed at that. I was fairly sure Delores had a crush on Joe as well, seeing as last week's muumuu had been a muted affair in shades of green, not a speck of glitter in sight.

"Let's have dinner before it burns. Then I can take

you to bed and play hide the sausage."

The delicious aroma of tomatoes and herbs wafted through from the kitchen, making my mouth water. Dinner sounded good because I needed the energy if Joe planned another night like last night. I'd struggled walking around the office a little today, but the delicious soreness was worth it.

"What are you cooking?"

"Pasta with meatballs."

"With more meatballs for dessert?"

"If you like."

Joe wouldn't let me lift a finger to help, so I sat at the breakfast bar with a glass of wine as he chopped up basil. Then he started pacing, a frown marring his otherwise smooth forehead.

"What's up?"

"What did Dane say to you again?"

"Do we have to talk about it?"

"Just one more time."

I sighed. "Fine."

Cringing, I repeated it back to him, well aware of my lip curling in revulsion.

"How did Dane know I was cooking?"

"Uh, I don't know. I guess he just assumed."

"Have you ever told him I cooked?"

"No."

"Then it's a pretty big assumption to make. Your home, your kitchen. How many men would take over?"

The accountant ordered food in or we ate out. The viscount got his personal chef to prepare most of our meals.

"Not many, I suppose."

Thor leapt out of the way and onto my lap as Joe

vaulted onto the kitchen island and stared at the ceiling, hands on hips.

"What on earth are you doing?"

He reached out and poked at the light fitting, then scraped at something with his fingernail. "Son of a bitch. That little fucker."

"What? What's going on?"

"That bastard's put a camera in here. He's been watching us."

CHAPTER 19

"DANE'S WHAT?" EVEN to my own ears, my voice sounded detached, flat.

Joe hopped down and pulled me tight against him. "Shhh, it's all right. It'll be all right."

"It's not all right!" I shrieked, and Thor leapt off my lap with an anguished howl. Loki joined him as they shot out of the room with Beyla bringing up the rear, hopping on her cast. A chill shuddered through me, starting at my ears and running through every limb until I couldn't stop shivering. Dane had been watching Joe cook in the kitchen, which meant he must also have seen what else we did in there this morning. I ran to the sink, where I threw up the remains of lunch as Joe held my hair back and kept whispering it would be okay.

No, it wouldn't.

A stranger had watched our most private moments, and goodness only knows what he'd been doing while he did so.

"What do we do?" A worse thought struck me. "What if he recorded...you know..." My gaze flicked towards the kitchen island. "That."

"I'll call the police. This is bigger than a neighbour with an odd streak now. He's blown it up into full-on lunacy."

An hour later, Joe cuddled me on the sofa as a

splintering crash came from the hallway. The police had arrived, and with no sign of Dane and no answer from his doorbell, they'd broken in. And things only got worse. Shuffling noises sounded from above as they clambered around in my empty loft.

"Have you ever been up there?" Joe asked.

The female police officer standing by the door came over and sat in an armchair.

"Never. The hatch was painted over when I moved in, and I figured there'd be spiders, so I never got it fixed. Besides, I was o-o-on my own, s-s-so I had plenty of space."

I hated crying in front of Joe, but I couldn't hold my tears back. That man had invaded my safe place. My *home*. Joe rubbed my back as I curled into him, trying to soothe me, but inside I felt numb.

A policeman appeared in the doorway, the one who'd arrived first forty minutes ago after Joe called 999. I wasn't sure it counted as an emergency, but they seemed to be taking it pretty seriously.

"Did you find the camera?" Joe asked.

The copper hesitated, and I knew from his expression it wasn't good news. "We found several. In the kitchen, the lounge, the hallway, all three bedrooms, and Miss Jenkins' en-suite bathroom."

Oh my... I didn't even have words for it. Dane had seen everything. *Everything*. Every intimate moment I'd shared with Joe from the second he arrived. Hell, before that when I'd pleasured myself in bed just thinking about him. When I'd drawn him, our first kiss, the moment he'd torn my damn trousers off.

"The cameras were all equipped with transmitters, and it looks like they fed into a laptop in Mr. Becker's dining room. We'll be getting one of our computer experts involved to see what he did with the videos. Whether he uploaded them anywhere."

I choked, but I'd already thrown up everything inside me before the police arrived. The thought that pictures of me doing such private things could be floating around in cyberspace left me barely able to breathe. What if my colleagues saw them? What if somebody told my parents?

"Just get that man locked up," Joe said.

"We're looking for him, sir, but London's a big place. We'll also need to get a statement from you and your girlfriend about everything that's happened. You mentioned Mr. Becker's been displaying some disturbing behaviour?"

"He's been fixated on Cate. Kept leaving her gifts every day."

"How long has this been going on?"

"As long as I've known her. How long, beautiful?"

"I never really spoke to him until I went to the gym downstairs and he was in there. He bugged me until I left and he hasn't left me alone since. Five weeks and, uh, two days."

"You're certain of the date?"

"Yes." Two days after I met Joe.

"We should be able to confirm that when we watch the recordings."

Marvellous. I'd never be able to look any of them in the eye again.

"Have you heard any odd noises?" the policeman asked. "He'd have had to drill the holes at some point."

"No, nothing, but I'm out at work all day. Wait. I did notice something. There were little bits of white grit a few days after I first talked to Dane, on my bed, the kitchen island, dotted around on the carpet. I thought it was just cat litter. I changed brand and the mess stopped."

"That'd be when he finished drilling the holes."

"I realise that now."

"I'm afraid we'll need to seal this place off and pull it apart. Is there someone you can stay with tonight?"

"I can't go to my parents'. Mother would go mental."

"How about Marie?" Joe asked.

"She's only got a one-bed flat."

"A hotel?" the policeman suggested.

"I've got three cats, and one of them's got a broken leg."

"I might know a place," the policewoman put in. "A friend of mine works at a hotel and they allow pets. Would that work?"

I nodded. Anything to get out of this house of horrors.

An hour later, the cab pulled up outside the Reuben Hotel. Joe helped me out, and a uniformed lady rushed out with the doorman to help with our luggage—two bags and three cat carriers.

"Mr. and Mrs. Streeter?"

"Close enough," Joe said.

"Martina said you'd had a bit of a trauma tonight. I've upgraded you to a deluxe room, no extra charge."

Her kindness made me burst into tears again. "Th-th-thank you."

"My pleasure. What lovely cats you have. I've got a British Shorthair myself."

She chattered about her pet as she led us up to our

room on the second floor, and I did my best to join in, desperate to maintain a facade of normality even though the last thing I felt like doing was talking. Once I'd admired the three velvet cat beds and the complimentary hamper of kitty treats, she backed towards the door.

"If you want to stay any longer, just phone down in the morning and we'll sort something out. It's zero to dial reception."

I let the cats out to explore then slumped back on the bed, watching as Thor headed for the food bowl, Loki sat on the windowsill, and Beyla curled up and closed her eyes. If only I could sleep that easily.

"How are you holding up?" Joe asked.

I felt too drained to try and put a brave face on things. "Not great," I admitted. "I loved my flat. It was the seventh place I looked at, the only one I felt comfortable in straight away, and I put an offer in the same afternoon. Now he's ruined it. I felt so bloody happy yesterday, and he's tainted those memories."

"We'll fix it. We can make new memories."

"And you're all mixed up in my mess too. I wanted to give you somewhere nice to live, not put you at the mercy of some perverted voyeur."

"I made just as much mess as you did last night, so we're in this together, wouldn't you say?"

"I know this is so new, but I don't want to lose you," I whispered, voicing my biggest fear.

"I'm not going anywhere, I promise. Come on, let's get some rest. We can start unravelling this in the morning."

"Don't you have to work?"

"I texted the boss on our way over here and

swapped to the evening shift."

Joe tucked me under the duvet and somehow, snuggled up in his arms, I managed to drift off.

***

Of course, nightmares of Dane came flooding back the next morning, and when my alarm went off, I buried my head under the duvet again.

"I can't face work," I mumbled.

"Can you take the day off?" Joe asked.

"I'll call in sick."

I'd never done it before, but I didn't feel too guilty, not after Sally took three days off because the beautician accidentally spray-tanned her the wrong colour. She refused to be seen in public again until she'd successfully exfoliated several shades of orange.

"Shall I ask the hotel to extend the room booking for another night?"

"Make it a week. I can't face going home anytime soon."

He leaned forward and kissed me softly. "Whatever you want. I'll see if I can get a couple of days off, but I can't afford to take the whole week."

"I'll be okay here by myself." I tried to smile, but it didn't work out so well. "Honestly."

Only when the afternoon came, it became obvious I was lying. I'd gone from independent to ridiculously needy overnight, and when Joe went to leave, I turned away to hide my tears.

Predictably, he noticed. "I'll stay."

"No, I don't want you to get into trouble."

"Then why don't you come with me? The cats will

be okay on their own for a few hours."

"Won't your boss mind?"

"Nah, he's cool. But you'll have to change out of your bathrobe. And not into yoga pants, or I might have to poke someone's eyes out."

"Will there be many women there?"

"Nope. And the ones who do go tend to be tougher than the men."

I felt a little apprehensive walking into the warehouse-like building, especially as it didn't seem to be in the best part of town. A group of youths hanging around outside had made me shrink back behind Joe, but when we walked past, they'd only given him a fist bump.

A blonde on reception grinned at Joe then looked me up and down with undisguised curiosity. I couldn't help giving her the once-over too, especially the full sleeve of tattoos on her left arm. She gave me a flat smile before she blew a bubble with the gum she was chewing and held out a letter to Joe.

"This came for ya, hun." She held out an envelope. "And Davey rang to say he's running ten minutes late for his session. Delays on the Northern Line."

"Thanks. Lindsey, this is Cate, my girlfriend. Cate, meet Lindsey, our gatekeeper."

His girlfriend. A glimmer of light penetrated the darkness surrounding me. Lindsey held out her hand to shake, and I couldn't take my eyes off the dragon tattooed across her knuckles.

"Like it?" Another bubble popped. "That one's new."

"Very impressive. Did it hurt?"

"Like hell."

"Is Jimmy around?" Joe asked her.

"Over by the cages."

Joe took my hand and led me deeper into the cavern, heading towards a pair of giant mesh enclosures. In the right-hand one, two men were beating the crap out of each other while a giant black man watched from the sidelines. He turned to look at us as we got closer, and I realised he was older than I first thought. In his late fifties, at a guess, maybe early sixties.

"Cate, this is Jimmy. He owns this place with his wife, Jackie. Jimmy, Cate's my girl."

A delightful shiver ran through me as he staked his claim once again. I held out a hand, but Jimmy bypassed that and pulled me into a hug.

"Uh, pleased to meet you," I mumbled into his massive chest.

"You look sad, child. I'm guessin' this isn't a social call." There was no judgement in his tone, only concern.

"I'm having some problems with my flat at the moment."

"Arsehole of a neighbour installed cameras in her bedroom ceiling."

"You take care of the problem?"

"He left before we found them, and he hasn't been home since. The cops are searching."

"They got leads?"

"Not when I spoke to them before we left. Can Cate stay in the break room? Her flat's crawling with cops, and I didn't want to leave her alone in the hotel."

"You work here, you're family. That makes Cate family, and we always look after our own." Jimmy turned and bellowed into the gym. "Amanda, get your ass over here."

The prettiest girl I'd ever seen emerged from a side room and sauntered over, wearing a sports bra and the type of tiny shorts I'd never have the confidence to pull off, even if I'd had the figure for them. Up close, she looked like she'd been airbrushed, but when she focused on me, her eyes had a hard edge to them that made me inch closer to Joe.

"We've got a problem needs fixin'," Jimmy told her, then repeated our conversation.

"What's the neighbour's full name and address?"

"Dane Becker," Joe said, and I shuddered at the mere mention of him as Joe gave her the details of Heron Court.

"Consider it dealt with," she said, then disappeared back to the depths of wherever she came from.

"That's my girl," Jimmy said, smiling as he watched her leave.

"Thanks," Joe said quietly and got a nod in return.

"Like I said, we look after our own."

Joe wrapped an arm around my waist and steered me across the gym. A few men working out cast curious glances in our direction, but nobody spoke. If I'd taken Joe into Berkeley, Rogers and Smyth, the email servers would have crashed two minutes after we walked through the door. And Sonia would have had a stroke. But here, there was only the sound of fists hitting leather and the *clank* of weights as Joe pushed open a door marked Staff Only and motioned me through. The room beyond smelled of sweat, and someone had left a pile of peanut shells on the table, but apart from that, it was tidy and more importantly, safe. Joe settled me into an armchair and touched his lips to mine.

"You'll be okay?"

"Who was that woman?"

"I've seen her around from time to time. Jimmy treats her like a daughter, but I've never asked for any more details." He gave me a sheepish look. "Truth be told, she makes me nervous as hell."

"Me too."

Joe gave me one more kiss before he headed for the door. "Good thing she's on our side, then."

CHAPTER 20

WITH THE NUMBER of scarily muscular men popping in and out of the break room, I felt safe enough curled up on the sofa there to get the little sketch pad out of my handbag and draw a few quick studies of Joe from memory. I'd got into the habit of carrying it with me after I realised how much the simple act of picking up a pencil relaxed me.

Joe brought us both sandwiches when he had a quiet moment and found the remote control for the TV on the wall so I could watch a movie instead of sports, and before I knew it, he was waking me up to go home.

"Oops. I can't believe I fell asleep."

"I can. You fidgeted all night last night."

"Sorry."

Joe leaned his forehead against mine and pushed a stray lock of hair behind my ear. "You were in my arms. That's the only thing that matters. Are you ready to go now?"

I nodded as he took my hand. "Thor's probably sulking by now."

Back in the hotel, I still felt numb as I sat on the chair by the window with Loki perched on my lap, demanding attention. Joe took the seat opposite and emptied his bag onto the table, then tossed his dirty workout clothes into the corner.

"I'll go back to the flat tomorrow and pick us up fresh clothes if the police are done. Unless you want to go back home?"

"I can't face it yet. Not the flat and not work. I'll call Reggie and get him to bring the files I need."

"You can sit at the gym again tomorrow if you want. Nobody minds."

He shoved his sweatshirt back into the bag, and I caught sight of the envelope the receptionist gave him earlier caught in the folds. A black logo graced the bottom right-hand corner—a set of scales alongside the words Drayton Phelps LLP.

"What's that?"

"It doesn't matter."

"Oh."

It stung more than I cared to admit when he brushed me off. We may not have known each other for long, but I'd been open about everything with him, and the idea of him keeping secrets hurt. It must have shown on my face because he knelt in front of me, hands resting lightly on my waist.

"That's my mess, beautiful. You've got enough on your plate without getting involved in my problems too."

"The property thing?"

He nodded.

"Maybe I could help?"

"It's over now. I'm gonna write back to the lawyer and tell him to drop the case. Meeting you's shown me I can't keep living in the past, and I'd rather focus on having a future together."

"What happened? Will you at least tell me that?"

"You really want to know?"

"Back in law school, I read case files for fun."

"Let me get a glass of wine first. Even thinking about it makes me so damn angry."

"Can you make it two?"

Wine turned into dessert from room service. Sod the diet—sometimes only ice cream and chocolate brownies would do. Joe had shoved the letter to one side while we shared a bowl heaped with calories, but now it came back to haunt us.

"So," he said.

"So."

"It all started before I was born. An elderly lady in the village needed some renovations done on her house, or so the story went, only she couldn't afford to pay. My grandpa felt sorry for her and fixed up her roof, and in return, she signed over a piece of land. A couple of acres in all. Not much to look at—just a field with woods at the end and a tiny pond. Me and Craig used to play there when we were kids, and he fell in one day. Shit, his mum was furious when he got home dripping with duck weed. Anyway, Grandpa passed, then Mum, and the land came to me."

"Where was the land?"

"Stonebridge. A little village near Oxford. The place where I grew up. I didn't touch the land when I inherited it, hadn't even set foot on it since I turned eighteen, but when Freya needed help, it was the only thing I had left that was worth anything."

"So what happened? You sold it?"

"Yeah. I went to school with this guy, Paul, and he friended me on Facebook a while back, so I knew he was a property developer. When I needed to sell, I asked him to do me a valuation."

"Two acres? How much?"

"I'd watched a few of those property programs, so I knew it would be worth more if someone could build on it, but he said no chance. Greenbelt, planning policies, local opposition, that sort of thing. Reckoned it was only worth its grazing value."

"Let me guess—he got it wrong?"

"Worse. The bastard said there was no market for paddocks and the like back then, but he'd take it on to help me out because his daughter wanted a pony. Fifteen grand he paid me, right before my last tour to Iraq."

"That's cheap, even for grazing land."

"When you've got nothing, it sounds like a hell of a lot, believe me. But then a couple of weeks after Craig's funeral, I drove through the village on my way to take his stuff from Iraq back to his parents, and they're building a whole housing estate there. Seventy houses. Paul already owned most of the land, and he needed my bit for access. Without that, his part would have only been good for grazing fucking horses."

"A ransom strip."

"A what?"

"A ransom strip. That's what they call it when you own the key to a new development. Around Oxford, if you'd sold two acres with planning permission, you could have multiplied that fifteen thousand by twenty. Maybe thirty. But a ransom strip? You could have named your price."

"Yeah, I know that now. He ripped me off, and when I asked him what he was playing at, he just laughed in my face and said I'd chosen to sign the contract."

"He took advantage of a man grieving for his mother and trying to care for his sister."

I hated him already.

"World's full of arseholes, Catie."

"But you got a lawyer? What did he say?"

"Pretty much what Paul Campbell did—that I'd signed the contract. I didn't exactly have the money to fight that battle." Joe sighed heavily. "I'm tired of it all. So damn tired. Like I said, it's time to forget it and move on, because if there's a chance of a future with you, I don't want to fuck that up."

"You couldn't mess it up if you tried." I nodded at the letter. "What's in that?"

"Nothing exciting. Just the lawyer asking if I want to carry on racking up a bigger bill." He wadded it up and threw it in the bin. "But the answer's no. I want to take you to bed instead."

I glanced involuntarily at the ceiling, then forced myself to put Dane out of my mind. Over twenty-four hours had passed since I'd had a Joe-induced orgasm, and I needed another one.

***

"Why does he keep looking at me?" Joe whispered.

He'd made love to me slowly and sweetly last night, ghosting his lips over mine as I fell asleep in his arms. Then when we woke up this morning, he'd got a little frisky, but before his tongue could work its magic, Thor had jumped up on the nightstand and fixed Joe with his beady glare.

"I think he's hungry."

"So am I."

"Maybe if I get up and give him some kitty crunchies..."

Joe swung his legs over the edge of the bed. "I'll get him the kitty crunchies, and then I've got a new plan."

"What plan?"

He grinned at me over his shoulder. "I promise you'll enjoy it."

"It" turned out to be shower sex, choreographed by Joe into a delicious dance of teasing fingers followed up by a frenzied fuck at the end. He had to carry me back to bed because my legs wouldn't work anymore.

Even then he didn't stop. My wet hair spread out over the towel he'd draped on the pillow as he stroked his hand up and down my body, pausing every so often to whisper dirty thoughts into my ear.

"What if housekeeping walk in?" I asked. "I've had enough of people watching us to last a lifetime."

"I'm putting the Do Not Disturb sign on the door. We've got all day. Well, until three. I've got an evening shift again."

Four more rounds with Joe and I no longer knew what time it was, where I was, or even my own name, and I groaned when he rolled out of bed and began to get dressed.

"Are you coming with me today?"

"I can't move. You broke me."

That got me a kiss and a smile. "Stay here and sleep, then. I'll text you when I'm on my way back, and we can order something for dinner."

"Mmm." No, my mouth didn't work anymore either.

My eyelids grew heavy as Joe gave me one last smile and slipped out the door. That man was everything to me now. Everything. I loved him.

***

I thought I'd sleep all evening, but it was still light when Loki batted a paw against my cheek and miaowed.

"All right, I know you're feeling neglected. I'll get you new toys, I promise."

Because anything Dane had left would be going on a ceremonial bonfire as soon as I got home. A smile spread across my face as I imagined dropping his bloody coffee machine out the window. I could almost hear the crunch now. Thor lay on the windowsill, plotting his escape, as Beyla limped over and rubbed herself against my legs.

"Hey, sweetie. You're looking better every day."

I petted the cats as I surfed through the TV channels, but despite having over fifty to choose from, there was nothing I wanted to watch. Perhaps I could try drawing? I plucked an apple from the complimentary fruit bowl and began to sketch, studying the angle of the stalk, the reflection of the street lamp outside on its polished skin. It was no good. I couldn't concentrate. I gave up and bit into the apple, relishing the sweetness on my tongue. Although it wasn't as delicious as the taste of Joe I'd had earlier.

It was only when I went to throw the core away that I remembered Joe's letter, still sitting in the bottom of the bin. Curiosity piqued, I unscrewed it and smoothed it out on the table. Yes, I knew I shouldn't have done it, but I was a lawyer. I made my living out of nosing through the details.

But Joe was right—the letter itself wasn't interesting at all. A simple pro forma asking if he wanted Mr. Phelps to keep the case open or archive the file. But the case itself both intrigued and angered me. Who was Paul, and how could he have done something so horrible to a man who'd once been a friend? Before I could stop myself, I opened up my laptop and bashed out a short email to Joe's lawyer. Would he be available for a little chat?

CHAPTER 21

I SHOULD HAVE gone into work, but I couldn't face it. Not yet. After seven years, three or four sick days wasn't too much to ask, was it?

Well, somebody thought so.

My phone buzzed at nine thirty with Reggie's name, and I resisted the temptation to send it to voicemail.

"Are you okay? Berkeley said you've still got food poisoning, but Sally reckons you're having your appendix out, and I also heard a rumour you're pregnant."

Oh, for goodness' sake. "Uh, it's actually none of those."

"Then what happened? Did your gym dude wear you out? Don't worry, I haven't told anyone about him."

I gave him a condensed version of Dane's antics, finishing with the news that he was still on the loose. When Joe spoke to the police first thing, they reckoned he'd seen the activity around Heron Court and bolted. Now they were waiting for him to turn his mobile phone back on so they could work out where he'd gone. Wouldn't it be ironic if he ended up at the homeless shelter?

Reggie let out a low whistle once I'd finished. "Whoa. That guy's whacked. No wonder you don't want to go out."

"It's just for a few days. He can't hide forever."

"Do you want me to bring any work over for you? Cookies? Candy? A gun?"

"Reggie..."

"Okay, okay, I was kidding about the gun."

"Could you scan over paperwork from the Hanover case? Or courier it? I'm at the Reuben Hotel, room 306."

"Yeah, I'll sort it out."

"Thanks."

"Cate?"

"Yes?"

"Just look after yourself, okay. Take whatever time you need and ignore Berkeley's grumbles. He's only complaining because you're the best lawyer here and he's lost without you."

Reggie's words brought a tiny smile to my face, and my gaze wandered to the sleeping form on the bed. "Don't worry, I intend to."

Not only did I not feel up to facing my colleagues, the decadence of a room-service breakfast with a hot man was something I could get used to, especially when he didn't put on a shirt first. Or trousers. And when he pushed his plate away and leaned back in his chair, I could see the outline of his cock through his tight underpants, or manties, as Marie called them, and I got hungry all over again.

"What time are you going to work today?" I asked. *Please say much, much later.*

"Not until three, but I thought I'd go over to the flat first and see how the cops are getting on. I need to fill in the holes in your ceiling too."

"I should come with you."

He leaned in and squeezed my hand. "No, you stay here. If the place is a mess, I don't want you seeing it."

The lawyer in me was tempted to argue, but I also wanted to check my emails without him leaning over my shoulder. "Okay."

"Okay?"

"Just hurry back."

That cheeky grin I loved so much popped onto his face, complete with dimples. "Promise you'll do one thing for me while I'm out?"

"Anything."

"Lose the knickers."

***

The instant the door closed behind Joe, I dived for my laptop. Would Mr. Phelps have replied to my message? Curiosity burned away at me, and my desire for justice stoked the flames.

Hallelujah! Apart from a lunch meeting between one and two, he was available for a chat. I glanced at my watch. Ten to one—would he answer now?

The phone rang once, twice. "Stanley Phelps."

"It's Cate Jenkins. You sent me an email this morning."

"I did indeed. I'll admit I was surprised to receive your note earlier—Mr. Streeter never gave the impression of being flush with money, and hiring you to represent him can't be cheap. While you're on the phone, I must say I was very impressed by your talk at the Law Society conference last October. Riveting."

At least somebody had enjoyed it. I'd puked in the toilet before I got up on stage, and even then, I couldn't stop shaking.

"Thank you. There've been so many changes in the property market lately it's hard to keep up."

"Indeed, indeed. So, Mr. Streeter?"

"Yes. Actually, he's become a friend, so this is more of a personal case for me. I offered to look into it for him."

Or something like that.

"Without receiving his formal instruction, I can't give you any confidential details."

"I understand that, and he's already told me about Paul and the land. I'm just trying to work out whether there's anything worth pursuing."

"The young man signed a contract, no doubt about that, but Campbell's a fishy character. I don't know what it's like in London, but out here in the countryside people talk, and it's not the first time he's pulled a trick like that."

"Interesting."

"And if that's how he works, I bet it won't be the last."

"I'm certain of it. If I get Joe to send you over a release letter, would you be able to send me your files?"

"A lot of what I have is merely rumour and conjecture at this stage. Look, I'm busy tomorrow but if you can get the letter, how about we meet for lunch on Saturday? I'll bring the files; you can bring that sharp mind of yours."

Oh dear. How on earth was I going to explain this to Joe? No idea, but I couldn't turn down Mr. Phelps' offer. "That's very kind of you. Shall we say twelve thirty?"

"There's a great little pub just along the road from

me. I'll have my secretary send you the details."

As soon as he hung up, I consulted my old friend Google. Paul Campbell, of Campbell Associates, had been a key player in several large developments in the Thames Valley over the last few years, and judging by the articles about them in local newspapers, none of them had been popular. The development in Stonebridge had outline planning permission at the moment, and the residents in the village were fighting against the detailed project—Campbell did indeed want to put seventy houses there as Joe said, plus three blocks of flats, a shopping centre, and a bowling alley. His website made a huge deal out of the park and community centre he'd offered as a platitude, but the overall picture was monstrous. It would destroy the picturesque village.

I'd become so engrossed in stories about property feuds I didn't notice how much time had passed until a knock on the door just after five.

"Who is it?" I hadn't ordered anything from room service, and housekeeping came while I was eating lunch.

"Me."

"Reggie?"

"I brought your files."

I hurried over to the door and let him in. Thank goodness I hadn't yet heeded Joe's instruction to remove my underwear.

"You didn't have to come over with them yourself."

He shrugged. "Anything to put off going home for a bit."

What was he talking about? Reggie never spoke about life outside work, other than his obsession with

Star Wars and a desire to visit the Kennedy Space Center. "Things aren't good?"

"Mum's got a new boyfriend."

"You don't get on?"

"Not really. Didn't like the last one either, but at least he had a job."

I opened the door wider, feeling sorry for the kid. I'd had no idea. "Come in and show me what files you've brought. I'll get room service to send up some coffee."

Reggie bent to pick up the bag he'd brought with him while I hastily shoved my dirty clothes under the bed. The poor boy would be scarred for life if he saw what I wore for Joe under my jeans and T-shirt.

"Shall I move these papers?" he asked. "Are they for work? Paul Campbell? I've seen his name somewhere before." He chewed his lip and stared up at the ceiling. "When I first joined the firm, Berkeley had the interns doing a load of filing. There was a Paul Campbell named in a property dispute. Something about a planning committee. I thought all those cases were closed?"

And this was why I loved Reggie. The kid had a memory like a computer as well as skills with the coffee machine.

"Can you remember the name of the case?"

"Grande vs. Northbury District Council, but I never read the details, only the front page."

"Can you find me the file?"

"Yeah. It was before we started scanning everything, though. I'll have to go down to the archive tomorrow."

"You're a star. And, uh, do you think you could not

mention it to Mr. Berkeley?"

"Why?"

"This is more of a private matter."

"You're poaching clients?" His eyes widened. "You're leaving?"

"No! A friend's having a problem, so I'm helping him out. Only he doesn't know I'm helping him out."

"Him? Gym guy?"

I sighed and collapsed overdramatically across the table. "Yes. Bloody hell, this is such a mess. He told me to leave it alone, and he'll be back soon. I've got to get all these papers tidied away, then somehow get him to give his old lawyer permission to talk to me without Joe dumping me or yelling."

Reggie patted me on the arm. "Hey, it'll be okay. Are you coming into the office tomorrow?"

"No, I might as well sack off the whole week. At least I'm not lying when I say I feel sick."

"I'll bring the Campbell file round tomorrow, yeah?"

"What would I do without you, Reggie?"

The moment he left, I dived for the minibar, poured two small bottles of white into a plastic wine glass, and knocked back the lot.

CHAPTER 22

I WAS BEGINNING to like this whole morning sex thing, although my enjoyment of Joe's cock was tempered slightly by the overriding dread that in the near future I'd have to confess about my phone call to Mr. Phelps.

"You okay, beautiful?" Joe asked as he peeled the condom off and tied a knot in the end.

"Fine. Why wouldn't I be?"

"You seem kind of subdued. Is it Dane?"

I grasped at that thought. "I'm worried he's still out there."

Joe kissed his way down my neck, and for a moment I forgot about everything.

"Don't think about him. I'll look after you, I promise. I need to finish sorting out your ceiling this morning, but you'll be safe here until I get back. Then you can come to work with me again if you like."

"Not today. My assistant's bringing some more files for me this afternoon, so I need to stick around. But I'm good, honestly."

"You can always talk to me, you know that?"

"Yes, I know."

But bringing up memories of the past he wanted to forget? He may have been understanding, but would he forgive me for sticking my nose into his life?

Sometimes I forgot just how little time I'd known him, and I had no past experience to gauge his reaction. I closed my eyes, remembering Marie's boyfriend-before-last. She'd wanted to go to an Indigo Rain concert, he said he didn't, she booked the tickets anyway, and I ended up with the second one after he dumped her. If he got that upset over an evening out with a band who were, by the way, freaking awesome, what would the repercussions be for my stunt with Phelps?

Damn lawyers and their bloody confidentiality agreements. If not for that, I could sneak off to Oxfordshire and see him on my own.

So many times I almost confessed that morning, but every time I opened my mouth the words stuck in my throat. I'd tell Joe when he got back this evening for sure. That would give me a few more hours to work out what to say, and possibly buy a flak jacket and get it couriered over.

"Be back as soon as I can, beautiful. Keep the bed warm."

"Shall I order dinner for us?"

"No, you eat. I'll grab a sandwich at work."

He'd almost got to the door when his phone rang, and when he looked at the screen, his brows pinched together.

"Who is it?" I asked.

"Police." He put the phone to his ear. "Joe Streeter."

I couldn't hear the other end of the conversation, but Joe smiled and switched to speaker.

"Cate's with me. Can you say that again?"

"We've got Dane Becker under arrest."

Thank goodness. I sagged against Joe, and he held

me up with an arm around my waist.

"Where? How did you find him?" I asked.

"Well, a funny thing happened. Two men carried him into Brick Lane police station, handcuffed him to a pillar, then left before the desk sergeant could ask any questions."

What the...? My mind raced back to the blonde woman in the gym. Did she have anything to do with it?

"Good thing you recognised him," Joe said.

"Our mysterious helpers wrote his name and the crime reference number on his forehead in permanent marker."

Joe choked back a laugh, and I buried my face against his shoulder as I did the same.

"You're not planning to let him out anytime soon, I hope."

"He's been remanded in custody. One of my colleagues will be in touch with details of the court case, but I wanted to let you know right away."

"Much appreciated."

"You have a good evening."

Once Joe had put his phone back in his pocket, he hugged me properly. "We can relax and enjoy the weekend now."

Something like that. "Looking forward to it."

"Save me a glass of wine?"

"Absolutely."

After he'd gone, I slumped against the door, which Loki took as an invitation to climb onto my lap.

"What am I gonna do, boy?"

Nothing. Not even a purr.

Reggie was smiling when he arrived an hour later, brandishing a bagful of files as well as a pair of cups from Starbucks. I shoved thoughts of Dane and his coffee habit to one side. At least Reggie knew I always drank espresso.

"Got it, boss, plus I ran a few searches and found some other interesting stuff."

"You had time for all that?"

"The senior partners are at a golf tournament today. Sonia's telling everyone you've gone for liposuction, by the way. Just thought you should know."

Wonderful. Yes, I could do with losing weight, but at least I didn't need a personality transplant, unlike some people. "Thanks."

"No problem. Are we setting up at the table?"

I ordered a plate of snacks, and Reggie ate one French fry after another, smothered in ketchup, as he tapped away at his laptop with his other hand. Meanwhile, I flipped open the Grande file and began to read.

Marlene Grande had wanted to buy a wreck of a house in Northbury village, only she got stuck in a bidding war with one Paul Campbell, which she won. Then she hit problems because she couldn't get planning permission for the renovations she wanted to do, and Campbell got pushy, offering to take the place off her for a lower price. I squinted at Mr. Berkeley's spidery scrawl in the margin. *How does he think he'll get planning permission to convert Arndale House into flats if Marlene isn't even allowed to rebuild the garage three feet wider?* He'd underlined "three feet" twice, his habit when he thought a point was ridiculous.

And to be fair, it was. Why was Campbell so keen to spend £1.2 million on a property mired with planning problems? Unless of course he knew those problems wouldn't apply to him.

Luckily, Marlene Grande appeared to be a tenacious lady, because she refused to give in, and according to Mr. Berkeley's file note, she informed Campbell she'd turn the place into a Halloween house of horrors and use it once a year to throw a bloody good party before she signed it over to him. Faced with that logic, the chairman of the planning committee had backed down and allowed her to renovate as she saw fit.

And Campbell took his fight elsewhere. He seemed to win more battles than he lost if his publicly available accounts were to be believed. Last year alone Campbell Associates cleared over a million in profit.

"Check this out," Reggie said. "He's coining it in, but his wife seems to be spending it. She totalled her Ferrari in January then got arrested for drink-driving."

The news website showed a picture of the wrecked car above one of Mr. and Mrs. Campbell at a party, wearing their finery. He didn't look like a creep, and I guessed that was partly why he was so successful. If I hadn't met Joe, I'd have given Campbell a second glance. Mind you, Dane hadn't been ugly either and look how that turned out.

"She probably suffers the hardship of having a chauffeur now," I muttered. Bitter? Yes, of course, when she was spending Joe's money to maintain her alcohol habit.

"It's a tough life. Did you tell your bloke what you're doing yet?"

"Nope. I'll have to bite the bullet later. Or maybe tomorrow, seeing as I need to go and visit his lawyer at lunchtime."

"Why don't you try to soften the blow by doing something nice for him? You know, to take his mind off it."

I nearly choked on my tea, but when I thought about it, Reggie's idea did make a certain amount of sense. "I guess. I think I've got a set of my good underwear with me."

It was Reggie's turn to splutter. "Good grief, Cate! You're my boss! I don't need to hear about that. I meant, why don't you take him out somewhere posh for breakfast or turn the trip into a weekend away?"

Oops. "Oh. Yes, of course. A weekend away. Why didn't I think of that?" As if he could read my thoughts, Thor miaowed at me then sat on my foot. "But we can't do that. The cats."

Reggie shrugged. "I can cat-sit if you want? I like the moggies, and it'd get me out of the house for a bit."

"Is your mum's boyfriend still giving you trouble?"

"He sits on the sofa all day watching football, and nobody's allowed to change the channel. I've missed three episodes of British Bake Off in a row now."

Who knew Reggie was a closet cookery fan?

"Well, Joe fixed the holes in my ceiling today, and I've got Netflix and Sky, so if you want to camp out in my flat for the weekend, then be my guest."

"Deal."

Would the promise of sex be enough to win Joe over? I had some major sucking up to do.

CHAPTER 23

"TWO DAYS OFF, and guess what I want to do. Or rather, who?"

At Joe's whispered words, I went from zero to soaking in ten seconds, and when he pushed his hips against me from behind, he was hard already. One hand came around to cup my breasts while the other reached between my legs, and the feel of his lips on the back of my neck made me press into him and shudder.

"I was never a morning person, but I think I've changed my mind."

I'd often pretended to be asleep when the accountant started his days with emails and herbal tea, but Joe's offer of dirty words and an enormous cock made me want to dance round the room singing "Oh, What a Beautiful Morning."

Right after he'd impaled me, obviously.

The rip of foil was swiftly followed by a delicious stretch as Joe nudged inside. I'd never get used to how good that felt. I never wanted to. Each time with Joe was better than the last.

And his words when he came inside me and wrapped me up in his arms made me melt.

"I love you, Catie. I know it's soon, but I can't keep it bottled up any longer."

My vagina set off party poppers while my heart

basked in a warm glow. Only my head spoiled the party with one little word: Phelps.

Even so, the words rolled off my tongue. "I love you too."

A pause. "Why do I sense a 'but' coming?"

"Uh..."

"You just tensed up in my arms, beautiful. What's wrong?" He loosened his arms and moved back a few inches. "Shit, I should have kept that to myself, shouldn't I?"

Oh, hell, I had to tell him. I rolled over to face the music.

"I did something that you won't like."

"Something with Dane?"

"No! The only thing I want to do with Dane is run his private parts through a shredder."

Joe winced. "Remind me never to get on your bad side. Look, whatever you did, it can't be that awful."

"I called your lawyer."

"Stanley Phelps?"

Eyes shut, I nodded. "I got the letter out of the bin."

I'd expected an explosion, but what I got was a hug. "I told you, it doesn't matter. Freya's got two years left at uni, my loan'll be paid off in a year and a half, and this nightmare'll be over. The last thing I want is for you to waste your time on a hopeless cause when you could be spending it with me."

"You're not angry?"

"It would take a hell of a lot to make me angry with you. I know you only want to help, and that only makes me love you more."

I pressed myself against him and hooked a leg over his hip, relieved beyond words. But the bright-eyed law student who'd gone into the profession in search of justice wouldn't give up. "Phelps reckons you're not the first person Campbell's done this to, and I know it might be futile, but I want to make his life just a little bit uncomfortable."

"Dane's caused you enough stress already."

"But this isn't stressful. It's my job, and I'm good at it."

"It'd feel like I'm using you."

"But I know you're not." I managed a tentative smile. "Phelps wants to meet with me for lunch. Will you be cross if I go?"

Joe blew out a long breath. "No."

"I thought maybe you could come with me? Not to the meeting, but for a weekend in the countryside. I haven't been out of London in ages."

That got me a smile. "A better idea. How are you planning on getting to his office? Do you have a car stashed away somewhere?"

"On my second driving lesson, the instructor rested his hand on my thigh and I crashed into a traffic light."

It had been red, so at least I'd stopped. And I even had the presence of mind to slap the pervert before I stormed off to the nearest Tube station, vowing to take public transport from that moment on.

Joe chuckled. "Served him right. Were you okay?"

"Fine, except I never finished the course."

"A no to the car, then. Hang on, what about the cats?"

"Reggie offered to cat-sit."

"You really thought this through, didn't you?"

"Sorry."

Joe kissed me on the nose. "One day, I'm going to

marry a lawyer, and she's going to be smart, and sweet, and beautiful, and she's also going to drive me crazy. And because of that, I'm going to love her even more."

Huh? My brain seized up at the "M" word. "What?"

He smiled the smile that would have had me stripping off my underwear if I'd been wearing any and rolled into a sitting position.

"One day. Not yet. Not until I can give her everything she deserves."

When I lay there like an overcooked noodle, staring into space as I tried to process the enormity of his words, he leaned over and tapped me on the ass.

"Come on, let's hire a car. Maybe I'll do dirty things to you in the back seat."

"I love you."

***

Two hours, one blow job, and a hasty breakfast later, we'd checked out, dropped the cats off at Heron Court with Reggie, and were speeding up the M40 motorway in a rented Honda. The back seat would be a tight fit, but it was the best vehicle we could find at such short notice.

Eight-year-old Cate, who'd walked Barbie and Ken down the aisle every day after school complete with confetti and flowers stolen from the vase in the downstairs hallway, was mentally picking out her wedding dress, while grown-up Cate desperately tried to focus on what to say to Phelps.

I knew law and Reggie was a genius when it came to research, but neither of us was familiar with the local area. Getting a feel for Campbell's operation would help enormously.

"Still time to back out," Joe said, a note of hope in his voice. "We could head straight for the hotel and start our dirty weekend early."

"I can't. I need to do this."

He brought my hand to his mouth and kissed it. "Then I'll be by your side."

Stanley Phelps was a kind-looking man whose three-piece suit and cravat made me feel under-dressed. Relics from a bygone age decorated the walls in the pub he'd chosen for lunch—the grille off an ancient tractor, black-and-white photos of rolling hills, faded rosettes from the county show—and some of them looked to be almost as old as the man himself.

We shook hands, his skin dry and papery, and he motioned Joe and me into seats opposite him at a snug table in the corner.

"Pleased to meet you, Miss Jenkins."

"Likewise. This is a lovely village."

"Aye, apart from that blight on the landscape as you drive in."

He was referring to Joe's land, now surrounded by metal fencing proclaiming the arrival of the new development. "It's all a mess, isn't it?"

"That it is. It's not that the locals don't want any new housing—we need some—it's the scale of the place. A new pub, that's his latest idea. He wants to put in one of those fancy places with a dance floor and loud music."

"Are you serious?"

He pushed a file towards me, an inch-thick pile of sheets in a faded orange folder, some of them handwritten in cursive script. An old-school man. I flipped it open as a waitress wandered over, pad in hand.

"You want to see the menu, Catie?" Joe asked.

"Could you just order something for me?"

I made a terrible dining companion as I flipped through the file, blocking out the low murmur of conversation from Joe and Mr. Phelps. Wow. Campbell sure was a nasty piece of work. His replies to Phelps were terse and rude, and then he'd stopped answering altogether. In the meantime, the scale of his development grew and grew, supported by a district planning committee headquartered in the next town who, Phelps noted, had never even been to visit the site in question.

So, why were they so keen on the building project?

I scanned through the list of members, and one name in particular caught my eye. Rasmussen. The surname of the committee chairman who'd given Marlene Grande so much trouble with her attempts to gain planning consent in a village thirty miles away. I flipped through my briefcase until I found my own notes from yesterday.

Dammit. Close, but no match. Marlene's antagonist was Harry Rasmussen, while the people of Stonebridge were having trouble with David. But even so... That was a flipping unusual surname.

"What do you know about David Rasmussen?" I asked Mr. Phelps.

"He's not a popular man around here. The local rugby team are talking about burning his effigy at their next Guy Fawkes party."

"What's his history? Has he put through many controversial developments?"

"I understand he was responsible for allowing a new shopping mall in Great Haseley. They built it right over a cemetery. And rumour has it he supported a big housing estate near the river. Smack bang in the middle of a flood plain. It's an insurance claim waiting to happen."

"Has he been on the planning committee for long?"

"A few years, I think."

"Has he ever used the name Harry?"

Phelps gave me a quizzical look, one bushy eyebrow quivering like an anxious caterpillar. "Not that I know of. Why? Are you onto something?"

"I'm not sure. The name Harry Rasmussen came up on another case Campbell was involved in, but I can't say too much about that. Client confidentiality. But I'll have a nose around."

"Be sure to let me know if there's anything I can do."

"Of course."

Lunch arrived, quiche for me, and I relaxed a little as conversation turned to village life and the upcoming harvest festival. Before I knew it, we'd bid Mr. Phelps, or Stanley, as he insisted I call him, goodbye, and Joe practically carried me to the car.

"This hotel you've booked had better have a sturdy bed."

Five stars, secluded, and our room even had its own terrace with a hot tub. Yes, it was a splurge, but I hadn't taken a break since the accountant dumped me a week before our planned trip to Norway. I'd been too depressed to go alone and stayed at home with my good friends Ben & Jerry instead. A night of filthy sex with Joe—okay, another one—was exactly what I needed, and maybe a small bowl of ice cream too.

But first I had to email Reggie.

CHAPTER 24

AT ELEVEN IN the evening, my phone buzzed with an email. I rolled sideways to the nightstand and pressed my thumb to the fingerprint scanner, but nothing happened, probably because my hands were all pruney. Joe had kept me naked in the hot tub for over two hours, even while we ate the selection of desserts I'd ordered from room service.

"I should sell my apartment and buy a house," I told him. "Then we could put one of these in the garden."

He'd laughed and nuzzled my ear. "We can make do in the shower."

I'd been joking when I said it, but the heaviness I felt in my stomach at the thought of going back to Heron Court was all too serious. Would I ever feel secure there again?

Those thoughts churned in my mind until Reggie's message provided a welcome distraction. First a picture of the cats, Beyla curled up on his lap, then an update on his afternoon of research.

Harry and David Rasmussen are brothers, both on planning committees, and they both have day jobs— Harry works behind the counter of a builder's merchant and David's an accounts assistant. But you know what? They both live in really big houses.

Reggie had even tracked down photos, and unless they had another income stream, there was no way they could have afforded those places on their salaries. Hell, I couldn't even dream of them on mine.

Seemed Reggie had already thought of that.

Guess who built those houses? BC Property and JD Construction, and those are fronts for... Go on, guess.

He'd attached the companies' annual returns showing the sole shareholder of each as a Jersey-based trust, coincidentally the same trust that owned one Campbell Associates.

"Gotcha!"

I may have shouted it a little loudly, because Joe rolled over and opened one eye. "You do, but I need sleep. You wore me out."

"Sorry."

But I was too buzzed for sleep. I hurried over to the tiny desk in the corner and hauled out my laptop so I could read through the files more easily. Reggie had found eight developments connected to Campbell that had been given planning approval in the last year by committees chaired by the Rasmussens, all in the face of local opposition. One shady property developer, two bent council officials.

The question was, what could we do about it?

Back in law school, my favourite professor gave me one important piece of advice, a quote he'd borrowed from Sun Tzu: know your enemy and know yourself, and you can fight a hundred battles without disaster. Sun Tzu and Joe may both have fought their battles on the field, while mine took place in more civilised surroundings, but the same principles still applied. They used swords and guns, whereas words were my weapons.

And to defeat Campbell, I had to find out more about him. With that in mind, I made myself a cup of coffee and began to compose a letter.

***

"Ready to go?" Joe asked the next morning.

"I'm not sure I can still walk."

He picked me up and threw me over his shoulder, so damn strong, and I shrieked.

"Put me down! People will see up my skirt if you take me out like this."

"You're right." Grinning, he paused in front of the mirror opposite the bed. "That view's for my eyes only. What time do we have to check out, again?"

"Ten minutes."

He set me back on my feet and smoothed my clothes down. "I'll take my time with you later."

Back in the car, I relaxed in the passenger seat as Joe fiddled with the SatNav on my phone. "Want to find a pub for lunch on the way back?"

"Of course. And could we just make one other quick stop?"

"Shopping? I thought you weren't keen on that."

"No, Campbell's office. I want to deliver a letter to him so I know for sure it's got there."

The nice lady at hotel reception had printed it out for me while we chatted about her new puppy.

Joe sighed but nodded anyway. "Anything for you."

As I expected from my knowledge of the man, the offices of Campbell Associates were visibly ostentatious. Set back from the road in a converted neo-Georgian house, Paul Campbell's domain boasted an air of class and legitimacy—not so much an illusion but an outright lie. The small lawn behind the car park was perfectly manicured, edged with a few late-blooming flowers clinging on until the first winter frost. What did surprise me was the light on in one of the upstairs windows as Joe swung the car into a space behind a compact Hyundai. A face peered out, and as I got to the door with my letter, it swung open. The lady standing there was a good foot shorter than me, bundled up in a woollen coat and a thick knitted scarf. The end came almost to her knees.

"Oh. I thought you were here to fix the radiator, but you don't look like a plumber."

In my old flat, the bathroom tap had dripped for six months before the landlord got his act together and fixed it, and it drove me mad.

"I'm afraid not."

She peered hopefully behind me. "And him?"

"No, he's not a plumber either."

"What's the problem?" Joe asked, wandering up behind me.

"Uh..."

"The radiator in my office isn't heating up properly. It's cold at the top and Mr. Campbell's plumber's as reliable as a politician."

"We're only here to drop off a letter."

She gave us a weary smile and held out a trembling hand. "Never mind. I can take it for you."

I handed it over. "I'm surprised there's anyone here on a Sunday."

"Not out of choice, let me tell you. But Mr. Campbell wants his monthly accounts, and the finance manager walked out last week. I'm the only person left who knows how to do them."

The way she said his name, it sounded like she didn't care for him much either, and no wonder if he was making her do somebody else's job as well as her own.

"It doesn't sound as if he's the easiest person to work for."

"Between you and me, I'm counting down the days to my retirement. Seventy-three left."

I wanted to hate her because she worked for the enemy, but dammit, I couldn't, and it seemed Joe felt the same.

"While we're here, I could take a quick look at that radiator if you like?"

"Would you? You're a true gent. I'm Margot, by the way."

"Joe and Cate."

She opened the door and beckoned us into the inner sanctum. The inside was as beautiful as the outside, and if I hadn't been so angry with the man who owned it, I might have enjoyed looking at the decor more. As it was, Margot led us up a wide staircase to the second floor and into her office at the back. Bloody hell, it was freezing.

"This room never gets the sun," she said. "There's the radiator, and I've brought up the toolbox."

While Joe fiddled with spanners, Margot waved me into the seat next to her desk and shuffled over to a filing cabinet where a kettle sat on a tray next to a tin of biscuits.

"Tea? Coffee?"

"Coffee would be lovely. Black for me, milky for Joe.

Isn't your coffee machine working either?"

"Oh, we don't have one of those. Mr. Campbell makes the staff bring our own refreshments."

"What, teabags too?"

"We have a rota. Of course, now one of us has left we'll have to redo that. More work."

Wow. Campbell made Mr. Berkeley look positively delightful. "Here, we stayed in a hotel last night and I picked up all these little biscuits from the tray in our room. You can have them."

She glanced up at the ceiling. "Someone was looking down on me this afternoon, sending me you two. Most days I barely talk to a soul. Mr. Campbell doesn't stand for idle chatter."

And she seemed like such a nice lady too. I glanced over at her computer and caught sight of the photo of two cats taped to the bottom of the monitor. Perhaps we weren't so different?

"Are those your cats?"

"Ah, yes, my babies. Sylvester's seven and Finnegan's a year older. I owned Fin's mother too, but Sylvester crawled onto my doorstep as a kitten and never left."

"I'm up to three now. They're all rescued, but Beyla literally fell at my feet when she got hit by a van."

By the time Joe got the radiator working again, I'd had my fix of cat gossip for the month and Margot had opened up her Facebook and shown me photos of all the moggies she'd ever owned, even an old black and white of her childhood favourite. If not for the situation, I'd have made a new friend.

"The radiator just needed bleeding," Joe said. "It should work fine now."

"Can I tempt you to another coffee?" Margot asked.

I wouldn't have minded, but we had a long drive back. "We'd better get going, but it was lovely to meet you."

"I'll make sure that letter goes on Mr. Campbell's desk first thing tomorrow morning."

"I'd be very grateful. Take care of yourself, Margot."

"You too, dearie."

Joe opened the car door for me, ever the gentleman.

"Now we wait," he said as he slipped behind the wheel.

After years as a lawyer, I was used to the process, but this time it was personal and my veins hummed with nervous energy as I buckled my seat belt.

"Yes, now we wait."

CHAPTER 25

ON MONDAY, THE office was full of chatter about the upcoming Team Weekend. Every year, the senior partners liked to arrange a bonding session so they could remind us of the importance of making them all as much money as possible. If we'd had a profitable year, they took us somewhere nice, like Barcelona or Euro Disney, but this year we'd barely scraped budget, hence the jaunt to the Lake District to rough it for two days.

Sonia and her cronies were gathered around a laptop at the kitchen counter, shopping for outdoor clothing on their phones in between watching videos of men in army fatigues posing for the camera.

"This jacket—blue or green?" Sonia asked.

"Green would blend into the surroundings better," Linda said.

"Since when is blending in a good thing? I'll get the blue."

I'd almost forgotten about the dreaded trip until a reminder flashed up about the pair of hiking boots I'd been watching on eBay. Joe had agreed to come with remarkable grace, and he'd even offered to sort out whatever equipment we needed, which meant I could grab an espresso and get on with some work rather than comparing the price of camping stoves on the internet. If I needed to cook, we were all doomed anyway.

Even with Joe beside me, I still dreaded going. I'd never exactly been sporty, and the thought of gallivanting around the countryside at the mercy of the British weather made me wish for appendicitis, or perhaps a particularly nasty bout of flu. Anything but this flipping excursion. Rumour had it we'd have to sleep outside and hunt our own food too. Good thing chocolate couldn't run because that was all I'd be catching.

Reggie, bless him, had offered to cat-sit again, and he'd also been doing more research on Campbell. By the time my darling assistant had finished, I'd know the man's inside leg measurement, the name of his first teacher, and what he liked for breakfast. And maybe, just maybe, how many of his developments he'd got approval for by bribing members of the planning committee.

I'd hoped to get a reply from Campbell early in the week. Thanks to Margot's promise, I knew he'd received the letter, but by Thursday I hadn't heard a peep—no phone call, no email, not even a letter via the good old postman. Mr. Campbell, it seemed, had decided to ignore me.

And that meant I needed to think about my next move.

I was still pondering when Joe was out at work on Thursday evening. He'd tried to swap to as many daytime shifts as possible so we could spend more time together, but sometimes the rota didn't work out in his favour. Still, he loved his job and I loved him, so we lived with it.

I'd just sat down to dinner—okay, a bowl of cereal—when my phone rang.

"Hello? Is that you, Cate?"

"Who is this?"

"Margot. You remember, we met on Sunday?"

What on earth did she want? "I could never forget you. How are the cats?"

"Not enamoured with the winter so far, but at least that means they don't go outside and leave little muddy footprints all over the furniture when they come back in."

"It has rained a lot this week, hasn't it?"

A long silence followed, and I waited for Margot to speak. For a moment I thought she'd hung up, but then she coughed.

"I gave your letter to Mr. Campbell like you asked. I didn't realise your Joe was Joe Streeter."

Busted. "Sorry. I considered mentioning it, but we were having such a lovely chat and I didn't want to spoil it by bringing up work."

"Yes, it would have rather put a damper on things, wouldn't it? Anyway, I'm calling because when Mr. Campbell read the letter, he just laughed and dropped it in the bin."

So that was why I hadn't heard from him. "Well, thanks for calling to say."

"I hope you don't mind, but I fished it out again to get your phone number. It never sat right with me, you know, the way he treated that young man."

Ah, a woman after my own heart. "It doesn't sit right with me either, which is why I'm helping him. And I don't think this is the first time Mr. Campbell has swindled somebody, I'm sad to say."

A long sigh. "No, you're right. So many times I wanted to walk out of there exactly like Tracey did last week, but the fact is there aren't many jobs around for a sixty-four-year-old woman with no formal qualifications."

"I'm so sorry."

"He wasn't always this bad, you know. Having money's gone to his head. He's got that ex-model wife now too, and she's always filling him with nonsense. Very materialistic, that one. Always has to be wearing the latest fashions and driving a brand-new car."

"Some ladies love that, don't they? Personally, I can't think of anything worse than traipsing around the shops every weekend."

Or trying to fit into some of the garments women passed off as clothes these days.

"I do most of my shopping on the internet. Saves my feet, plus the young man who delivers the parcels is ever so handsome."

"I love eBay. I furnished half my flat from there."

"Have you tried Etsy? When I retire, I'm going to open my own store and sell my crocheted animals."

"Ooh, could you do my cats?"

"I'm sure I could, dearie. Sixty-eight days and counting."

Ah yes, work. "So, do you think I should try writing to Mr. Campbell again? Or will he just throw that letter away too?"

"I think you should try again, but I want to give you something that might help with your problem first. You were so kind to me, and I'd like to return the favour."

Really? My heart started to beat faster. Margot wanted to help us? "Wow. Er, I don't know what to say.

What do you want to give us?"

"Emails. But I had to print them all out onto paper. Would you be able to meet me this weekend?"

Dammit! That bloody team-building thing. "Work's making us go on a survival exercise in the Lake District this weekend. Crawling through mud and catching our own food, that sort of thing."

"That sounds like something Mr. Campbell would do to us if it didn't cost money."

A giggle escaped. "Yes, it does, doesn't it? We've got to drive up north after lunch tomorrow ready to start at six a.m. on Saturday, so we could meet you in the afternoon if you're free?"

"I'll text you my address. Mr. Campbell's taken his wife to Marbella for a long weekend, so I can sneak out early."

***

The senior partners gave us all Friday afternoon off so we could make our way north to our doom. In the morning, I overheard Mr. Berkeley asking his PA whether his new golf glove had been delivered yet. Guess his idea of exploring the great outdoors was vastly different from ours.

But at five to twelve, I was ready to dash out the door after one last check with Reggie that he'd be okay with the cats.

"You've got Netflix, you've left me money for pizza, your freak of a next-door neighbour's been charged with trespass and voyeurism... I'll be fine," he said.

"I'd say call me if you need anything, but apparently they'll be confiscating our phones."

"Just go."

"Okay, okay."

I scurried out to the lift, and before I knew it, Joe was picking me up at the kerb outside. After the joys of the tiny Honda last week, I'd gone for something more in keeping with our trip to muddy hell and hired a Land Rover. Green, chunky, perfect for the country, and as an added bonus, it had a decent-sized back seat in case Joe felt like taking it for a test drive.

"I feel like I should be wearing tweed and carrying a shotgun," he muttered.

"As it happens..." I reached into my bag and fished out a flat cap, a late delivery to the office this morning.

Joe turned to me at a set of traffic lights and raised one eyebrow. "Seriously?"

I wrinkled my nose. Maybe not.

He leaned over for a quick kiss. "Good thing I love you."

He loved me. I still had to pinch myself when I woke up next to him every morning, and the dirty looks I got from other women when they saw his arm around me would take some getting used to as well. But he was my future, as long as we could survive whatever Five-Star Survival had planned for us this weekend. I'd taken a look at their brochure, but it had been worryingly light on the details.

"Are we still stopping in Great Haseley?" Joe asked.

"Just for a few minutes."

"I still feel bad about you getting involved in all this."

"Honestly, don't. I kind of like lawyering, at least when Berkeley isn't making me do his photocopying for him."

The Land Rover rattled its way up the M40 while I fiddled with the radio. Why was it that as soon as we got past junction five, all the good stations disappeared? Eventually, I settled on Jack FM, a bizarre mix of cheesy pop and old classics. *Come back, London, all is forgiven.*

Margot must have been waiting at the door because when I knocked, it opened almost instantly.

"Come in, dears. I know you must be in a hurry, but I've made you tea."

And hats. She must have been up all night knitting those. Mine was a little on the large side, but I rolled the edge up, and Joe smiled like a trooper as she fussed around tucking his hair underneath a snazzy olive-green number as he sipped from a dainty cup.

"Lovely," I said.

"Don't want you two catching your deaths up in those mountains. The temperature got down to four degrees last night, but my office is cosy as anything now."

"That's wonderful news."

She pressed a fat envelope into my hands. "Here's what you came for. But you didn't get it from me, okay?"

"I promise I won't mention your name anywhere. And make sure you send me the link for your Etsy store when you get it set up."

"I'll be sure to do that, dear."

Out in the car, Joe reached over to clip my seat belt into place as I thumbed through the contents.

"Couldn't wait to get started, huh?"

"These emails are gold. Pure bloody gold. There's a whole trail between Campbell and both Rasmussens.

Campbell knew he'd get planning permission before he even put in an offer for your land."

"That bastard. He was all right when we were at school, but he's turned into a monster."

"And he's already doing it again. Trying to get a lady to part with her mother's old cottage so he can get access to the land behind." He'd offered below market price for a quick sale, and the letter was dated two days ago. The man had no morals whatsoever. "I'm going to take these bloody emails and stuff them up his arse."

"That's my girl." Joe reached over and twined his fingers through mine. "But first we have to get you through this weekend of bullshit."

CHAPTER 26

HOME SWEET HOME. Well, at least for one night, and it wasn't so much a home as a small hotel on the edge of a bloody great forest. With fifty of us going, we'd been divided among two establishments, and Joe and I had been lucky enough to get assigned to the same place as Sonia and her minions. Wonderful. Just when I thought the weekend couldn't possibly get any worse.

I locked the envelope full of papers in the glove compartment while Joe hefted our cases out of the boot. Despite a small detour halfway where we may have found a quiet car park to christen the back seat, we'd made good time, and according to the information folder in our room, the bar and restaurant would be open for another half hour.

"Do you want to get something to eat?" I asked.

He turned and waggled his eyebrows. I loved the new, more playful Joe.

"Thought we already did that," he said.

Ah, yes. My cheeks burned at the thought of the snack I'd eaten on the way. Sausage and meatballs. Delicious.

"I meant actual food."

"Just teasing. They don't do room service?"

"Apparently not."

It seemed everyone else had come up with the same

idea, because the tiny bar was packed with people from Berkeley, Rogers and Smyth. Every head turned to look at us as we walked in, and I fancied several of the jaws even dropped. On the outside, I was careful to maintain a neutral facade, but inside I was grinning like an idiot. Yes, ladies, I did manage to find a hot guy.

"Aren't you going to introduce us?" Linda squealed.

"This is Joe, my boyfriend." Yup, that smile just got wider.

At least until Sonia spoke up.

"I've seen you somewhere before."

Where? Where could she possibly have seen him? I glanced over at Joe, but he looked equally confused.

Then Sonia snapped her fingers. "Got it! You were in the shelter at St. Jude's when I volunteered there for one horrible evening. OMG! Cate, you've shacked up with a homeless person? That's a new low, even for you."

Beside me, Joe stiffened, and dead silence fell over the room. Even the barman stopped to watch the spectacle.

How could she? How could Sonia be so bloody mean? Of course, she hadn't picked up a sexy ex-army officer who just happened to have once spent a few weeks in a homeless shelter to bring this weekend, had she? No, it very much looked as if she'd ordered the twit fiddling with his phone beside her from the LL Bean catalogue. And her smug smile? That came from Bitches-R-Us.

"It wasn't like that."

"You didn't pick him up from the streets? With the amount you earn, I'm surprised you didn't hire somebody from a reputable agency."

Well, I'd come close, hadn't I? At least until I found someone much better. And what had I said to myself when Dane threatened to expose us before? That Joe's origins didn't matter. I loved him, he loved me, and we had our future to look forward to. Painful though the stares and whispers may have been, my colleagues' opinions were just that—opinions. And like armpits, everybody had them and some of them stunk.

I slipped an arm around Joe's waist and held him tight. "Sonia, I'm not sure you've ever experienced anything more than a passing infatuation with a man's wallet, but let me assure you that just like the animosity I feel towards you, my love for Joe is the real thing." She stared as I tugged Joe towards the door. "I think we'll go somewhere else. It's bad enough sharing airspace with you in the office."

I hated to retreat, but it was either climb into the car or claw Sonia's eyes out, and that wouldn't have looked so good on my CV.

Why did you leave your last job, Cate?

Because I blinded my colleague on a team-building weekend.

"Sorry about that," I said as Joe started the engine. "If I'd known she'd recognise you, I'd never have put you through this."

He turned to face me, and one side of his lips quirked up. "My lady's got balls."

Unable to resist, I reached into his lap. "No, the balls are all yours."

"No, those belong to you now, as does the rest of me. Come on, let's find some food before the real hell starts tomorrow."

***

I was still seething the next morning when I staggered out of bed. We'd eaten in a Chinese restaurant last night before sneaking back to the hotel at half past eleven.

"I can't believe that woman," I grumbled.

"You said that last night, and sadly the way she thinks is all too common. The other men in the shelter came back with horror stories each day. I was one of the lucky ones because I found work quickly, and then I met you."

"This whole weekend is awful. I should quit and become a flipping artist instead. I may be penniless, but at least I'd be happy."

"Something to aim for in the future, then." He gave me one of those grins. "I'll always model if you want to practise. Hey, maybe I'll even draw you one day?"

"Can you actually draw?"

"No, but that doesn't matter as long as you're naked."

I threw a pillow at him and he caught it, laughing. No matter how shitty things got, he always cheered me up.

"Come on, beautiful. Let's get dressed and find out what joys await us."

He'd chosen my clothes—thick socks, jeans and waterproof trousers to go over the top, a fleece top, and a sturdy down jacket—and as instructed, we'd left all our valuables in the safe.

"I'm hot," I said.

"Yeah, I know that."

"I meant from the clothes."

He bent to kiss me, sliding his hands under my top. I thought he wanted another quickie until I felt him slip something into my bra.

"What's that?"

"Your credit card. Shh."

"Why?"

"Trust me, okay?"

Once we'd laced up our boots—new for me, well-worn for Joe—we headed down to the restaurant for breakfast. Or not, as it turned out. Instead of the typical hotel fare of cereal, toast, fruit, and an assortment of fried stuff, a long table held a collection of bags with names on, one for each person.

What the hell?

A man dressed from head to toe in camouflage was sitting next to the bags, chatting with Becky and Sally, who'd abandoned their respective beaus and headed off in search of something a little more...rugged.

"Where's breakfast?" I whispered to Joe.

"No idea, but I suspect we're about to find out."

Camouflage guy stood up and thumped a fist on the table, making me jump.

"Ladies and gentlemen, welcome to your five-star survival weekend. I'm Duke Montgomery, your commander-in-chief for this challenge. For the next two days, you're not just going to step out of your comfort zone, you're going to take a running leap. In a few minutes, I'll divide you into teams, and with the assistance of one of my highly trained staff, you'll race each other from here to the village of Braywater, thirty miles away."

Thirty miles? He had to be bloody kidding.

"And here's where it gets fun, folks. You'll have no

phones, no money, none of the creature comforts you're used to. Everything you'll need is in those bags, so use it wisely. I won't pretend this'll be easy, folks, but that's not the aim of the game. Did I have an iPad when I fought against insurgents in Iraq? Did I carry a smartphone in my pocket when I took on the Taliban in Afghanistan? When I crossed behind enemy lines, all I had with me was my mind and body, honed by years of training and dedication..."

He droned on about the missions he'd been on, the enemy he'd "annihilated, destroyed," and the number of civilians he'd rescued from the brink of doom. I glanced up at Joe, and he rolled his eyes.

"Wannabe," he muttered under his breath.

Eventually, Duke shut up and introduced us to his cohorts, similarly attired but with the addition of greasy camouflage paint all over their faces. Our babysitter, or master-at-arms, as Duke preferred to call him, was a baby-faced Welshman who looked even less thrilled to be there than me. He couldn't have been more than twenty-two.

"I'm Daffyd. Do you want to introduce yourselves with a fun fact?"

We dutifully nodded, except for Becky's companion, who hadn't said a word so far. In a stroke of bad luck, Joe and I had also been stuck with Linda and boyfriend number three. Did he know about the other two?

"I'm Cate, and I've got three cats."

"Joe. I can play every Beatles song on the harmonica."

For a second I thought he was serious, but then I saw one corner of his lips twitch.

"My name's Linda. I have a first-class honours

degree in economics."

Yup, real "fun."

"Harvey Weston. I'm studying biological sciences and my dissertation's on the mechanics of sexual reproduction in frogs."

Fantastic. Well, maybe he'd meet some new friends out in the woods.

"Hi, everyone. I'm Becky. I've watched every single episode of *Made in Chelsea*." The guy with her shuffled nervously from foot to foot when everybody looked at him, and she giggled. "And this is Gianni. His English isn't so good."

Okay, one guess as to why she was with him. He must have other oral skills.

Daffyd looked at his watch. "Okay, I need you all to empty your pockets. No wallets, phones, or snacks. Duke says I have to check."

Good grief, it was worse than being back at school, when they used to search our bags for calculators before our weekly mental arithmetic tests. Linda sighed and put her phone down on the table while Becky clung onto hers like a lifeline.

"What if I miss something important?"

"Like what?" Linda asked.

"Uh, a flash shoe sale? Or a local sighting on celebgossip.com?"

Linda gently prised the phone from her fingers. "You'll survive for two days." She held it out to Daffyd. "These are going to be looked after, right? Because we're all lawyers, and we'll sue you if anything goes missing."

He swallowed nervously. "We'll look after everything, for sure. Now, we'd better get going because this is a race, after all, and we need to cover at least fifteen miles before we set up our camp for the night."

Becky sucked in a breath. "Camp?"

"Where did you think we were going to sleep?" Linda asked.

"I guess in another hotel or something. Maybe a bed and breakfast."

Daffyd adopted a tone meant to convey enthusiasm. "That's why they call this a survival course. It wouldn't be much of a challenge if we all schlepped up to a fancy resort, would it?"

"I don't want a challenge. I want a facial and a manicure."

None of us wanted to be there, so all we could do was make the best of it.

"Look on the bright side," I said. "The sooner we leave, the sooner we'll be able to go back to London."

CHAPTER 27

OUTSIDE, WE CLUTCHED our paper sacks like kids on the first day of kindergarten. Well, except Joe. He stood tall, but with an air of resignation about him.

"Right, let's all look in our bags," Daffyd said.

He appeared more nervous than anything else, which hardly inspired confidence.

We all emptied our goodies out into a pile, finding such delights as an aluminium cooking tin and a whole collection of canned goods without labels on them. Boy, I was really looking forward to dinner.

"We supply the basics. Anything else you need to catch or forage," Daffyd explained.

"Catch?" Linda looked a little green. "I think I just turned vegetarian."

To our left, Sonia's group set off down the lane, with her bringing up the rear while her bloke marched along at the front. Her discomfort made me feel marginally better, as did the fact that I wasn't on her team, so I wouldn't have to listen to her whining for two whole days.

Daffyd waved a piece of paper. "I've got the map. If we go right, we can take a shortcut."

"No, we can't," Joe told him. "You've got it upside down."

Well, this was a great start.

"I'm not even sure I can walk fifteen miles," I whispered to Joe as we headed off after Sonia and co.

"Don't worry. I'll take care of you. Trust me."

"I do."

But I still couldn't help feeling bloody miserable, especially when the first splashes of rain fell.

The weather only got worse as we slipped and slithered our way along a narrow path in the forest. At first, the trees sheltered us, but as the drizzle turned into a deluge, it torrented through the leaves above and fat drops soaked us through.

"This is fun," Linda muttered. "Not. At least Berkeley, Rogers, and bloody Smith's golf game won't be going much better."

"They'll be in the bar," Becky pointed out. "I need a freaking cocktail. Or a Jägerbomb. This weekend calls for Jägerbombs."

Linda's feet went from under her in the mud, but Joe caught her before she fell. "Easy. There's no hurry."

"It's impossible to stay upright on this path."

"Hang on a minute."

Joe reached down the front of his jeans and came back with a fancy-looking multi-tool in his hand. Seconds later, he'd sawn a branch into a walking stick for Linda to lean on.

"I can't use that. I'll feel like I'm a hundred years old."

"Would you rather fall over?"

Five seconds passed, then ten, and she reached out and took the stick. "If any of you tell Sonia about this, I'll never speak to you again."

That actually sounded like quite a good deal to me, but even so, I'd never say anything. Not to Sonia.

Daffyd had gone on ahead, but at the sound of our voices he turned back and stared at the handy-dandy saw in Joe's hand. "Where did you get that?"

"Found it."

Daffyd narrowed his eyes. "Really?"

"Yeah. In my pocket."

"I checked your pockets."

"Well, you didn't look hard enough."

I couldn't help giggling. "This is why I brought you with me, Streeter."

Daffyd looked at me, then back to Joe. "Streeter? Joe Streeter? Like, *the* Joe Streeter who won the Victoria Cross?"

He'd what?

"I only did what anyone else would have done."

"No way, man. You're a fucking hero. You saved, like, fifty people."

"But I couldn't save everyone." Joe's voice cracked, and I knew he was talking about Craig Collier.

I pointed along the track, opting for distraction. "Is that a deer?"

"Where?" Daffyd asked.

"Up ahead, to the... Oh, it's disappeared into the trees now. Shall we get going?"

Daffyd waved at Joe. "You should lead the way. I mean, you're far better at all this stuff than me."

I thought Joe was going to decline, but he shrugged and jerked his head at a side trail.

"Let's go this way."

"Are you sure?" I asked.

He grinned and gave my hand a squeeze. "Trust me."

After half an hour, we arrived outside the Badger

and Barrel, a quaint country pub that advertised the best pies in the north of England and claimed to serve sixteen different types of real ale. And hallelujah! It had a toilet.

Daffyd looked a little confused. "Where are we? I thought we were heading to Braywater?"

"We are. Via the pub," Joe informed him.

Suddenly it clicked why he'd hidden my credit card in my bra. "We're stopping for lunch?"

"I think we've earned it."

"No, no, no," Daffyd said. "This isn't allowed. We're supposed to be using our ingenuity to feed ourselves."

"We are. Look, if I got hungry out in Iraq and there was a chance to eat with the locals, we took it. We didn't head out to the bloody desert and start hunting rats."

"But what if Duke finds out?"

"I don't think anyone here's gonna tell him. Right?"

Five rather bedraggled hikers shook their heads.

Daffyd let out a resigned sigh. "Fine. But this wasn't my idea and I know nothing about it. Say, is that steak pie on the menu?"

Joe paid up front for our food at the bar, and the landlord let us have a table by the back door so we could slip out just in case Duke or any of the other teams turned up to spoil our meal. While we waited for the food, I made a beeline for the ladies' room, followed by Linda and Becky.

"I never thought I'd be so grateful for toilet paper," Linda said.

"Or a mirror," Becky put in. "My hair's full of leaves."

"Reckon you did all right with your Joe, no matter

what Sonia says."

I smiled inside the locked cubicle. "I know I did."

But it didn't hurt to hear Linda say it.

Out in the bar, our food had arrived, and a burger and chips had never looked so good. Joe usually stuck with something healthier, but I noticed he'd gone for steak today. I covered everything in ketchup and relaxed for the first time since we left London. An hour passed as we went for dessert as well, and once I'd scraped up the last of my chocolate mousse, my stomach was groaning and the idea of trekking through the woods again made me feel sick.

"What's the plan?" Daffyd asked Joe.

"Borrow the phone at the bar and sort out a hotel room for the night."

Daffyd might have been easy-going so far, but now his mouth set in a thin line. "You can't do that. Duke'll go nuts, and the goal for this weekend is to learn more about yourselves and find strength you didn't know you had."

"Duke's full of shit. Did you hear all that crap coming out his mouth back in the hotel? He said he'd served in Iraq under Brigadier Fieldhouse, but Fieldhouse never even went to Iraq. If Duke was in the military, I bet he spent his time scrubbing the mess hall floor back in Blighty. And as for goals, you know what mine is? To get my girlfriend safely back to London with the least trauma possible from some arsehole who's sent a bunch of office workers out into the wilderness without any proper equipment or means to communicate."

Daffyd shrank back in his seat. "I hear the Travel Inn near Kendal's quite good."

Joe leaned forward and patted him on the cheek. "See? Now we're working as a team."

Half an hour later, we squashed into the back of a people carrier as the taxi driver wound his way past the lakes and mountains. The scenery was quite picturesque now I didn't have to traipse around in it.

No, instead we got a double bedroom overlooking the car park, with a squeaky door and a television plagued by static. But compared to where I thought I'd have to sleep, the place was heaven. Oh, and Joe had remembered the condoms. Six of them. At least I'd look convincingly exhausted when we got to the finish line tomorrow.

***

Sunday brought more rain, and after a leisurely breakfast that didn't involve suspicious-looking canned goods, campfires, or nettle tea, we called another taxi to take us most of the way to Braywater.

"Now what?" Linda asked. "We go and find Duke? We'll win easily."

Joe shook his head. "I'm quite happy to bend the rules to make everyone more comfortable, but I draw the line at cheating to win. No, we'll find another pub for lunch, then walk round for a bit so we look wet and muddy."

And that was exactly what we did. I fell into a puddle, which helped, and Becky had taken a shower, so Linda and I added a few leaves and some dirt to her hair. Linda's biology student got distracted by a rare frog, and by the time we'd hauled him away from the pond it was squatting beside, it was time to head back and find Duke.

Seventh.

We came seventh. I didn't care, because the rest of the time Joe made sure I came first, including twice this morning.

Besides, the weekend wasn't a complete loss. Linda, Becky, and I had bonded over a shared hatred of all things outdoor, and while I couldn't see myself hanging out with them at the weekends, I had hope that my time in the office wouldn't be quite so unpleasant from now on. As long as I could avoid Sonia, anyway. Speaking of Sonia, where was she?

"Has anybody seen Sonia?"

Her date looked up from the score sheet he was studying. His team had won, and I got the impression he wouldn't have been happy with anything else.

"She went back."

"Oh." So she hadn't spent the night under the rain after all. I felt strangely disappointed about that.

Duke stood up on a chair and clapped his hands for silence. "Ladies and gentlemen, let me say how proud I am of all of you. We've got through two days of hell with only one minor injury, and now it's time for dinner and the medal ceremony. The bus is waiting outside, and I'm sure you'll all be glad to get a shower."

"What injury?" I whispered to Linda.

"Sally's boyfriend got bitten by a rabbit."

The coach driver gave us all filthy looks as we climbed on board, no doubt unimpressed by our attire. Didn't he know this was the country? Surely mud was to be expected? We got stuck behind a tractor, then a bunch of cows, and by the time we arrived back at our starting point, I was half asleep with my head resting on Joe's shoulder.

"You look worn out," he murmured as we pulled up outside our hotel.

"Why do you think that is?"

"I'd apologise, but I'm not sorry."

We'd got halfway across the foyer when a commotion by the front desk caught our attention. Sonia's boyfriend was berating the receptionist about something or other, and the poor girl was shaking her head as he leaned into her space.

"What's the problem?" Joe asked.

The arsehole turned around, hands on hips, then realised Joe stood four inches taller and backed down a bit.

"I can't find Sonia. She's not in our room, and this woman says she didn't come back yesterday," he said.

The poor lady tried to speak up. "I'm sure she didn't. I was on duty all afternoon and evening, and I'd have—"

"You're clearly mistaken. Where else would she have gone in this hotel?"

"I don't know. Only the bar, but it's just opened after cleaning and nobody's gone through the door."

"Well, I suggest you find your manager and start looking properly."

"What if she didn't come back?" I asked, and the receptionist shot me a grateful look.

"Nonsense. Of course she did."

Joe didn't look amused about the way the poncey git was talking to me.

"What exactly happened yesterday?" he asked.

"We got a couple of miles away and Sonia slipped over in the mud, then decided she was coming back here."

"And you didn't come with her?"

He looked shocked at the thought. "We were winning, and besides, it was uphill."

"So you let a lone woman walk off through the woods?"

"Don't judge me like that. I tried to stop her, but she wouldn't listen."

Wow. I'd thought Duke was a grade A asshole, but this idiot had him beaten hands down. Even though I didn't like Sonia, I still felt sorry for her if she'd been stuck out in the mountains on her own all night. When we'd left the Travel Inn this morning, there were still traces of frost on the ground.

Duke wandered in, and Joe waved him over. "You've got a missing woman."

"Huh?"

"Sonia left her group yesterday to come back to the hotel, but she never arrived."

Duke beckoned another man I recognised as the master-at-arms for Sonia's team.

"Did that scary lady go back to the hotel yesterday?" Duke asked.

"Yeah. She insisted she'd had enough."

"Nobody came with her?"

"She looked kind of angry. We figured she'd be all right on her own. We were only a mile or two away, and it was mostly straight."

"She might not have got here," I said.

The man didn't seem bothered, and I wanted to shake him for his lack of concern. Then Sonia for causing all these problems.

"You need to call the police and the search-and-rescue team," Joe said to Duke, who bristled at Joe's tone.

Duke didn't strike me as a man who liked being told what to do.

"She's probably packed up and headed back to London. I'm not calling out the emergency services when she's most likely sitting at home on the sofa."

"Without her phone or her wallet? Presumably those are still in the hotel safe?"

The receptionist nodded, and Joe stared down Duke.

"What if she's still out on the mountain? You want to take that chance?"

Duke sighed and looked at his watch. "That woman's a drama queen if I ever saw one. Fine. I'll send my own men out to look."

Really? Because if they were all as smart as Daffyd, their combined IQs wouldn't reach double figures, and as two of them walked out of the bar, they were already drinking beer.

"Fuck it," Joe muttered, shaking his head as Duke walked off. "He could be right. She could have been pissed enough to take off back to the city, even without her stuff."

"A woman never leaves her phone."

"Fuck it."

"What are we going to do?"

"You're going to relax in the hotel room while I go out to look for her, just in case."

"No way. If you're going, then I am too."

"Catie, it'll be dark in two hours. I don't want you getting cold or hurt."

"What about you? What if you get cold or hurt?"

"I've spent nights in places that make the Lake District look like a holiday camp. I'll be fine, and I'll take some of the guys with me to help."

"And me." I folded my arms.

"Catie..."

"You can drop me back here later, but I'm coming to help first."

After a quick conversation with our team, Harvey-the-frog-guy and Daffyd came with us to the Land Rover while Linda and Becky stayed in the hotel to try ringing Sonia's friends in London in case she'd gone back there. But when her boyfriend checked their room and found her suitcase still open at the end of the bed and her handbag in the wardrobe, it looked more and more unlikely.

Bloody hell, just when I thought I'd escaped the horrors the Lake District had to offer, fate stepped in with a reminder. At least we'd rented a 4x4 instead of that Honda again, because it meant we could drive most of the way, inching our way along the rutted tracks that wound through the trees. An hour passed with us peering into the darkening trees, calling out Sonia's name in the hope that she might be nearby. Even with the heater turned right up, my fingers and toes were still chilly.

And we found nothing.

"We need to head out on foot," Joe said. "Do you want me to drop you back first?"

"No, I'm fine."

I wasn't, but neither did I plan on admitting that fact. If Joe had to spend his evening hunting for my irritating colleague because he'd done me a favour by coming on this dumb team-building weekend, then the least I could do was share the pain. And yes, there was pain. My new boots pinched with every step, and my voice was hoarse from shouting.

Daffyd had brought torches for each of us, and as the sun dropped down behind the horizon, he handed them out.

"The batteries are supposed to last for four hours," he told Joe.

"If we're still out here in four hours, we've got bigger problems than batteries. Daffyd, you and Harvey take the path to the left. I'll go right with Cate. Don't go out of each other's sight, and check in every fifteen minutes on the phone. Got it?"

"Got it."

We'd been stumbling along for almost half an hour, sliding in mud and tripping over tree roots, when a weak voice answered one of my shouts.

"Sonia? Is that you?" I yelled.

"Over here."

Her voice came from the left, and Joe beat me to her. Sonia was sitting on the damp ground, huddled against the trunk of an old oak tree, and her pale face was a sharp contrast to the dark night.

"What happened?" Joe asked.

"I got lost, and then I fell and hurt my ankle. It might be broken. And I'm cold. S-s-so c-c-cold."

Joe had finally replaced the jacket he donated to Beyla, and now he shrugged it off and wrapped it around Sonia's shoulders. "I'll call for an ambulance."

"How will it get here?"

"You're only three hundred yards from the road. They'll bring a stretcher, and we'll carry you out."

She closed her eyes and leaned back against the tree

trunk. "I thought I was going to die here."

No such luck.

I squeezed her shoulder, trying to give her some support because even though she'd been awful to me, her ankle was the size of a football and she looked terrible, like she'd just received all the karma she'd collected over her adult life in one go.

"I'm sure you'll be fine."

She let out a low groan. "I'm never leaving London again."

That made two of us.

CHAPTER 28

BY THE TIME we got back to the hotel from the hospital, midnight had passed and dinner was nothing but a distant dream. All I wanted to do was go to bed, but as Joe and I crept through reception, the lanky frame of Smyth unfolded from a chair. Sonia's boss.

"How is she?"

"Exhausted, and she's suffering from hypothermia."

"And her ankle?"

Daffyd and frog-guy had got back to the hotel ahead of us and no doubt spread the news.

"A hairline fracture and ligament damage."

He winced visibly. "Ouch. Looks like she'll be needing some time off."

"The doctor said at least a week, and then she'll be walking with crutches for another five."

"What a pain." He shook his head, and his droopy jowls wobbled like a Bassett Hound's. "Excuse the pun. I had a chat with Berkeley and Rogers over dinner, and we decided it would be best if you stayed up here to drive her back."

Just when I thought my day couldn't get any worse.

"But we can't. I've got Mr. Harrington coming in tomorrow afternoon, and Joe needs to work. What about that id—her boyfriend?"

"He's already left. Something about a meeting

tomorrow morning. Berkeley will deal with Mr. Harrington, and I'm sure if your young man explains the situation, his employers will be accommodating. We'll reimburse you both for any out-of-pocket expenses." He patted me on the arm. "Look on it as a free holiday."

No, I looked on it for what it was—everyone else's strong desire not to be stuck with her for the six-hour trip down south. Tiredness got the better of me, and I couldn't help snapping a little.

"If you stick me in a car with Sonia for six hours, you'll be bailing one of us out for murder."

A hint of a smile flickered at the corner of his mouth. "Don't worry, Miss Jenkins, we have an excellent legal team at your disposal. Besides, Sonia's not that bad once you get to know her."

Really? Were we talking about the same person?

Smyth turned his attention to Joe. "You'll help the girl out, won't you?"

"If you're so fond of her, why don't you stay and do the honours?"

"Alas, I have to make an appearance at the Old Bailey, and the judge won't be too impressed if I don't turn up."

"Fine. But Cate gets the rest of the week off to recover from this debacle. This team-building exercise was the biggest crock of shit I've ever been involved in, and as a man who's served in three war zones, I know what I'm talking about."

"Mr. Duke will be receiving a strongly worded letter, rest assured."

"Rest assured," I mimicked as Smyth disappeared up the stairs on the far side of the foyer. "This is my worst nightmare. How can I bloody rest?"

"Because I'm gonna give you at least three orgasms, and tomorrow morning, we'll head out and buy a big roll of duct tape."

"For Sonia's mouth?"

"If she doesn't keep it shut. Or I could use it for your wrists if you're into a bit of kink." He wrapped his arms around me and trailed his lips along my neck. "The rota means I don't need to go to work until Thursday evening. I wanted to surprise you by repainting the lounge where the cops scraped it up, but it looks like we'll be spending the time in bed instead, seeing as you've got the rest of the week off."

Okay, it wasn't all bad. Six hours in a car with Sonia versus four days with Joe.

"And we can go out for a posh dinner tomorrow and Smyth can bloody pay for it."

"That's my girl."

***

The senior partners wanted an update on Sonia's condition, which meant we had to pay her a visit on Monday afternoon, although after the things Joe had done to me in the morning, it was me who needed the crutches, not her.

We found her in a private room, testing the firm's medical coverage to its limits with a widescreen television and complimentary fruit bowl. Her leg was ensconced in plaster from knee to toe, and the paper nightgown did nothing for her complexion.

"How are you?" I asked.

"All right." She eyed me up warily as Joe perched

on the chair by the window.

"Does it hurt much?"

"Not with the pills."

A row of bottles competed for space on the tiny nightstand, alongside a copy of *Cosmopolitan* and her Louis Vuitton handbag. Would any of them help with her personality disorder?

"How long do you have to stay here?"

"The doctors said I can go home tomorrow if there are no complications overnight. Five hours. They reckon I'd only have lasted five more hours if the temperature dropped again."

A tear rolled down her cheek, and I couldn't help feeling sorry for her.

"Don't think about it, okay? We found you, you're in hospital, and next week you'll be back in the office to make my life a misery."

That last bit just popped out, and I tried to smile and turn it into a joke, but it sounded all too serious.

"I'm sorry," she said, her voice quiet, sounding more like a child than the Sonia I knew and hated.

"Huh?"

"I'm sorry. I know I've been mean, but once I started, it was hard to change how I behaved. Everyone expected it from me."

"But why? Why even be like that in the first place?"

She shrugged and stared out the window at a flock of passing birds. "I went to an all-girls school, and that was how things were. You were either the hunter or the hunted, and for so long I was their prey. When I left that hellhole, I swore I'd never be at the bottom of the pile again, and I didn't know how to stay on top without putting other people down." Her tears were flowing thick and fast now. "And you've always been so bloody good at everything. The partners love you."

What the hell did they put in those pills?

"Uh, they like you too. Smyth told me last night you weren't such a bad person."

She choked back a laugh. "I'm not so bad? Berkeley told me you'd be having his job when he retires."

"He said that?"

"Yeah, he did."

"But he still asks me to do his photocopying."

"Only because he doesn't know how to work the machine. He tried to fax a document through the shredder last week."

I sank back into the chair next to the bed, confused. Why was Sonia behaving like a human being? It made me nervous.

"I don't get it. Why now? Why are you saying all this now?"

"It's been weighing on my mind for a while. And then you walked in with him." She waved a hand at Joe. "Did you know the volunteers at the shelter called him the homeless hottie? I was tempted to invite him out for dinner myself."

"I'd have said no," Joe muttered from his spot on the other side of the room, and Sonia stared down at the blankets.

"And I'd have deserved it. I'm sorry. For how I thought of you and how I treated you."

Hold on, did Sonia just apologise again? Twice in one day? She'd just used up her entire annual quota.

"When I was stuck out in the woods overnight," she continued, "I had so much time to think. Just think. I can't carry on like this."

"Then change," I said.

"It's not that easy. If I walked into the office next Monday and started being nice to everyone, people would probably have me sectioned."

"Then take smaller steps." Why was I even helping her? "Everyone grouses, but don't bitch about the people standing in front of you. If you feel the need to be negative, complain about the weather or last night's movie or politicians. They're always fair game."

"This is gonna be hard. I know I've got no right to ask, but will you help me?"

"How?"

"I don't know. Throw something at me when I screw things up?"

Like a hot cup of coffee? "Yeah, I guess."

"Thank you." She dropped her head back against the pillow, and her brows pinched together.

"Do you need the nurse?"

She nodded. "The good stuff is wearing off."

***

"Well, that was just about the strangest afternoon I've ever had to endure," I said to Joe on the way back to the hotel. "Do you think she was serious?"

He nodded as he steered the car along country lanes. "People do a lot of thinking when they believe the end is near. Sometimes it changes them for the better, sometimes for the worse. One of my sergeants came home from Iraq and joined the seminary. Another never got over what he saw and took his own life."

I wrapped my hand around Joe's on the gear knob.

"I'm sorry you had to go through that," I said softly.

"So am I. The whole world's a mess. All we can do is try to make the best of our own little corner."

"Perhaps this weekend didn't turn out so bad after all. I mean, apart from Sonia almost dying. If I can get on better with the girls in the office, I'll enjoy work more."

"Maybe we should send Duke a thank-you card?"

"Let's not go too far, eh?"

CHAPTER 29

SONIA STAYED QUIET on the way home, and by the time we drove around the outskirts of Birmingham, she'd fallen asleep in the back seat and my mind had found something new to worry about.

Campbell.

I got the papers out of the glove compartment and studied them as Joe whizzed along the motorway, accompanied by the dulcet tones of Frank Sinatra on the radio. We had the leverage we needed here—I just needed to work out the best way to use it. A little more research was needed before we tipped our hand as to what we had, and then I'd have to try for another meeting.

Margot must have spent the whole night printing this lot out. Pages and pages, and by the time Joe hit the A40, the count of Campbell's victims had reached double figures. The man had made millions out of other people's misery, picking on those already suffering hardship as his targets of choice. Joe had fallen right into his lap. The Rasmussens didn't seem much better —David had chaired two other planning committees in the north of England before he moved to Oxfordshire, and no doubt made a pretty penny out of both.

"What are all those papers?" Sonia asked on a yawn. "Not working again already? Smyth said he gave you the week off."

"Sort of."

She reached forward and grabbed a handful from my lap. "What's this? Paul Campbell?"

"Hey! Give those back! It's a personal matter." I twisted around, but she held them out of reach.

"Personal matter? You don't want to get mixed up with that prick. Yeah, yeah, I know I'm not supposed to insult people anymore, but honestly, the man makes it easy."

"You've met him?"

"Year before last. The Grande case. Campbell tried to ruin Marlene Grande's dream." Sonia shook her head—in admiration, it seemed. "Seventy years old, and she wouldn't give in. Berkeley brought me onto the team to negotiate Campbell's surrender."

"He gave up?"

"Not easily. He's a sly bastard. So, he's back again? What's he done this time? Swindled a pensioner out of her life savings? Or a grieving relative? Those are his speciality."

Should I tell Sonia what happened? On the one hand, she may have information about Campbell we could use, but I still didn't trust her. Not after all the years she'd tormented me.

In the end, Joe made the decision so I didn't have to. "Not a pensioner. Me."

In the rear-view mirror, Sonia's eyes widened. "Seriously?"

"Like you said, he targets those who are grieving and takes advantage of them."

"Someone died? Shit... I'm not good at this sympathy thing."

"I don't want sympathy. I want to forget Campbell and move on with my life, but someone very close to me has decided she wants to do something about it."

"Too right. Otherwise, Campbell will keep doing this until he's developed half of Oxfordshire. What's the story?"

I told her a condensed version, careful to leave Margot's name out of it. Sonia may have shown indications of joining the human race, but I still wasn't convinced she'd transition successfully.

When I finished my story, Sonia broke into a wide grin. "Well, I'll be damned. His own camp handed over the rope to hang him."

"I guess. I just haven't had much experience with the, er, hanging part."

"Honey, you're looking at the head executioner right here."

Didn't I know it? "I don't suppose you could give me some pointers?"

"I can do more than that. If it wasn't for Mr. Commando here, my body would be going cold in that bloody forest. We've both got the week off, right?"

"Uh, yes?"

"So we use the time to plan our case. You can teach me to be nicer to people, and I'll help bring out your inner bitch. Every girl's got one, trust me. You just don't let yours show very often."

"Are you serious?"

"Deadly."

She was deadly all right. I'd seen her reduce the CEO of a billion-dollar corporation to a quivering wreck before she'd even had her morning coffee. Maybe she could hang on to her nasty side for just a few weeks longer?

Joe shook his head and smiled as I reached a hand back for Sonia to shake. "Deal."

"Deal."

***

And so our unlikely alliance was born. Sonia and I spent the rest of the week studying everything we could get our hands on relating to Campbell and the Rasmussens, along with Reggie helping in the evenings. He'd made jokes about garlic and stakes when he first saw her sitting at my kitchen counter with Loki on her lap, but when he realised how hard she was trying to change, he'd added her coffee to the Starbucks run when he went to fetch mine.

Besides the notes from Marlene Grande's file, Reggie turned up complaints against Campbell going back for a decade. He'd started his dodgy dealings almost as soon as he left school. While Joe had been serving his country, Paul Campbell had started his chequered career by garden grabbing—building single homes or small developments on the excess land at the back of residential properties. A slew of accusations followed, everything from dubious valuations to misrepresentation of what he intended to build. A single lawsuit had been filed and dropped on a technicality, and two years later, Campbell had met David Rasmussen and expanded his ambitions along with both of their bank balances.

"This guy's a bulldozer," I said. "If anything or anyone stands in his way, he flattens it."

"It certainly seems that way." Sonia waved a file at

me. "Eighty homes built on a green field site, on a freaking flood plain. The whole development ended up underwater two years later, but he got some expert on climate change in to testify and wriggled out of the class action against him."

"How do we stand a chance?"

"Simple. He never plays fair, so we're not going to either."

And on Friday afternoon, Joe came home with a bundle of papers in a plain brown envelope and dropped them on the table in front of me.

"Amanda at the gym gave me these."

"What are they?"

"I don't know. I'm not sure I even want to know. But she said they might help us, and according to Jimmy, she's never wrong."

Sonia snatched the envelope and tore it open, with Reggie leaning over her shoulder as she began to read. It only took a few seconds for Reggie to step back with his hands over his face.

"Someone pass the bleach—I need to wash my eyes out," he wailed.

"What? What is it?" I asked.

Sonia grinned and slid a photo over to me. "Campbell's one sick puppy."

Flipping heck—now I knew why Reggie needed the bleach, and I was next in line for the bottle. The crisp picture showed Campbell on his hands and knees, naked, with his twig and berries hanging free while a leather-clad lady who wasn't his wife led him round on a sparkly dog lead. Another scary-looking lady—also not his wife—was spanking him with a paddle.

"What? How?"

Joe glanced down, and his eyes widened. "Like I said, I don't want to know."

"Can we use this? I mean, is it legal?"

Sonia snorted. "Legal? You think Campbell cares about legal? Too damn right we're going to use this. If his wife found out and wanted a divorce, how much do you reckon that'd cost him?"

Reggie glanced at his notes. "Campbell's estimated net worth is sixty million pounds."

I shook my head, feeling sick. "Who says crime doesn't pay?"

Sonia rolled her eyes. "We're lawyers, Cate. Crime always pays."

She did have a point there. "As long as Campbell pays too."

"Oh, he's going to pay, believe me. This meeting's going to be fun."

Just when I thought Sonia and I might not be so different after all, she proved me wrong. Her idea of fun made me want to throw up my lunch then catch the nearest flight to a non-extradition country.

***

Joe must have been nervous about the Campbell case too, but he still lent me his strength when nerves got the better of me every evening, mainly by distracting me from the files stacked high on my dining table.

"Time for bed, Catie."

"But it's only eight o'clock."

His eyes gleamed as he looked me up and down, those gorgeous blue pools I lost myself in every night.

"I didn't mean to sleep," he said.

"What about dinner?"

"I know what I want to eat."

A shiver ran through me, but I couldn't resist teasing, something I'd never felt brave enough to do with Mr. Calculator or the viscount. "Pizza?"

Joe was already dragging his shirt over his head, and I bit my bottom lip as the ridges of his abs were revealed. I still couldn't believe my luck every time I got to trace them with my tongue, eight rippling squares that spoke of dedication to his job. When we got our lives back, I wanted to draw him again. Maybe even frame my efforts and hang them on our bedroom wall.

"Pizza?" he muttered. "Not quite, but it begins with the same letter."

Ooh, the more Joe settled in, the dirtier his mind got, although we still had a way to go before he put on a leather collar to get his bottom spanked.

"How about pie? Or passion fruit?" I asked.

A growl rumbled in his throat. "Get naked, Catie. Your tits in that shirt have been driving me crazy all day."

I was only too happy to oblige.

CHAPTER 30

BY THE FOLLOWING week, we were ready. Sonia sent me an email on Monday morning, right after Berkeley stacked a week's worth of files on my desk and sauntered off whistling.

Meeting set for Thursday at ten. Campbell sounded nervous on the phone. Guess he remembers me.

Good. He should be nervous, because unless he agreed to our terms, we planned to release a dossier of his dodgy dealings to the press and every protest group he'd ever encountered. And we still had our ace to play —the photos from Amanda.

Wednesday evening saw me contract another mysterious bout of food poisoning, and on Thursday morning, I put on my best pathetic voice and called in sick. I might have felt guilty if I hadn't worked the equivalent of Thursday's hours already that week in unpaid overtime.

"All set?" Joe asked.

"All set."

At Sonia's suggestion, I'd worn a skirt suit, feminine but business-like, and dark red lipstick that Joe had already kissed off me three times.

"Go for hot but untouchable," Sonia had said. "I've spent years experimenting, and that's what scares them most. Plus, I wear glasses because it makes me look smarter."

Sonia 2.0 hadn't made a single crack about my weight and even went so far as to tell me I looked pretty on one memorable occasion. Okay, so she'd also accidentally said the new intern looked like a grasshopper on LSD, but she realised and backtracked the instant I held my hand up.

And Joe looked devastatingly handsome in his suit. I just wanted to peel him out of it, and if he gave me that smouldering look one more time, we'd never get to the bloody meeting. Although my stomach would be relieved about that. It had turned itself inside out so many times the food poisoning would have been a welcome alternative.

At some point, we'd need to buy a car, because having to keep hiring one was a pain, especially when I had an allocated parking space sitting empty outside. Today's vehicle was another Honda, but a larger model so the back seat could accommodate Sonia's cast. We picked her up on the way, and then we were off to Oxfordshire again.

"Just remember," Sonia told us when we pulled up outside the offices of Campbell Associates. "Sit up straight, don't fidget, and don't capitulate on anything if he speaks to you directly. I'll do most of the talking."

"I think I'm going to be sick. How can you smile about this?"

"Because I enjoy watching powerful men squirm."

She hobbled off, and I followed with Joe.

"I pity any man who faces her in the bedroom," he whispered. "I bet she's got a leather outfit and a whip stashed away somewhere. Probably she'd get on well with Campbell under different circumstances."

I choked back a laugh. "Good thing we didn't buy that duct tape, then. She might have enjoyed it."

Inside, Margot winked as she showed us into the conference room. "Good luck, dears."

I'd need it.

Fear gnawed away at me, and I did my best not to let it show as I watched Sonia tear Campbell into little pieces and stuff him through a mincer over his dishonest developments. Technical questions came to me, and she asked Joe a little about the history of his land, but apart from that, it was her show. By the time it came to the final negotiation, Campbell had shrunk three inches, and he kept glancing at the door.

"What do you want from me?" he asked.

Sonia smiled sweetly. "I thought you'd never ask. My client will settle for a reduced development on the land at the entrance to Stonebridge village and three point five million pounds."

I nearly fell off my seat. When we discussed it, she said she'd start at two point five and go down to one point eight. Secretly, I wasn't even sure we'd get that. Joe's fingernails dug into my thigh, and from the way his hand shook, he hadn't been expecting it either.

"When you say reduced development, how much are you talking?"

"No flats, no nightclub, no bowling alley, no shopping mall. A tasteful development of forty detached houses max, with plenty of open space. You know damn well you'll still make a healthy profit out of that, and we won't tell the world about your little arrangement with the Rasmussens."

"Forty private houses plus another ten affordable.

We have to include them, and you know we'll barely make two percent on those. The shopping mall stays, and I'll offer two million five for the land settlement."

Fuck!

But Sonia wasn't done. "We'll agree on the social housing, but no shopping mall. A small parade of shops would be acceptable. And we'll drop to three million three on the land. No lower. *You* know it's worth that."

"Three two."

"Three two fifty."

"Fine. Are we done?" He pushed his chair back, answering his own question.

Sonia smiled again, a hard thin line this time, and stayed seated. "Almost. We do have one other small matter to discuss."

Oh dear. I knew what was coming. Sonia had been cagey about her plans for Amanda's dossier, but no way had she forgotten about it.

"Define small," Campbell said.

"I'd say about four inches," Sonia said. "Although I needed to get my magnifying glass out to check."

She flicked the dog collar photo across the table, and all the colour drained out of Campbell's face. Not an easy feat when, according to Reggie, he spent one month out of every three sunning himself at his holiday villa in the Bahamas.

"W-w-what the hell is this?" Campbell stuttered.

"Another million."

His jaw clenched so hard I heard it crack. "You're blackmailing me?"

"No, Mr. Campbell, we're negotiating. Isn't this how men like you work?"

"You're going to regret this."

"We've got more photos, if you'd like to see them? My favourite is the one where you're getting your backside spanked with a ruler by a girl who looks barely legal."

Campbell stared at Sonia, his expression murderous, but she held his gaze without blinking.

"Would you like Mr. Streeter's account details for the money transfer?" she asked.

"If I ever see you again after today..."

"Keep your nose clean and you won't have to." She leaned over and tapped the photo. "I'd suggest not snorting that line of coke in the background. It's a dangerous habit. Do we have a deal?"

"Get out."

"Do we have a deal?"

"Yes, we have a fucking deal. Out!"

I managed to maintain a professional facade until we got to the car, but when Joe pulled into a lay-by around the corner, I began babbling like an idiot.

"Four and a quarter million pounds? Did I hear that right?"

Sonia grinned, deservedly so. "Am I good, or am I good? When Campbell started fidgeting and tapping his foot, I realised how nervous he was and figured I might as well go in big. Although I'm wondering if I shouldn't have asked for two for the ruler thing."

"I'm donating the money from the ruler thing to charity," Joe said. "It doesn't seem right to profit from blackmail."

"Holy shit," I whispered, but there was no point in asking Joe whether he was sure about his decision. Knowing Joe's ethics, it was the only decision he could have made. "Which charity?"

"The homeless shelter I stayed at. It'll make a big difference there."

"Charity?" Sonia asked. "Well, it's your choice. And I accept tips in handbags and cupcakes."

"I'll buy you a whole bakery," Joe said.

"Nah, I don't need all that—it'll go straight to my hips. But if we're talking handbags, I've got a weakness for Chanel, and my favourite colour is pink."

Lucky for me, Joe liked hips. And I loved, loved, loved Joe. This whole situation was crazy. I'd fallen for a penniless man with a good heart and ended up with a hot millionaire model who also cooked. Who said dreams never came true?

I let out a crazy shriek, somewhere between a banshee and a cat in pain, and the other two stared at me.

"Uh, I'm just happy, that's all."

Sonia peered at me over her fake glasses. "I'd hate to hear you unhappy. My eardrums would burst."

"I can't get over how insane this is."

Joe had been living out of a rucksack, and now he had the means to buy a mansion. Everything was different. He pulled back into traffic and a mile passed, then two, then three, before my initial euphoria gave way to something less pleasant. An iron band tightened around my heart as I considered the wider implications. What if this new Joe came to his senses and realised he could do so much better than me now?

"Don't," he muttered under his breath.

"Don't what?" I asked.

"I know what you're thinking, Catie, and nothing's changed."

"Everything's changed."

"Not the important things. Money didn't come between us before, and it won't in the future. You're it for me, no matter what our bank balances say."

He reached over and twined his fingers through mine, then brought my knuckles to his lips before resting our joined hands on my thigh as we headed down the motorway for the trip back to London.

"You're it for me too, Mr. Streeter," I told him.

***

The next day after work, I opened the front door and tripped over a gift-wrapped package on the floor in my hallway. So pretty—silver paper with a puffy pink bow and curly ribbon—but my first thought was *Dane*, and I almost threw it out into the corridor. But then I realised that not only was it inside my flat, it also had my name printed on the outside in Joe's handwriting.

A gift! For me! And not a freakishly sweet cup of coffee in sight.

I tore open the paper and found a selection of sketch pads and a deluxe box of art supplies—pens, pencils, paints, even a set of pastels, and all top quality.

"Joe?" I called.

"In the living room."

I headed in that direction. "Thank you so—"

The words died on my tongue as I took in the delicious sight of Joe reclining on the sofa, starkers. A single chair sat in front of him with an easel set up next to it, ready and waiting.

"I feel bad that you missed your art classes for the last two weeks, so I thought we'd play a game," he said. "You can draw all the things you want me to do to you, and then I'll do them."

He'd really thought this through, hadn't he? Not only had he bought the art supplies, he'd chilled a bottle of champagne in an ice bucket and picked up a big box of chocolate truffles. And now my knickers were decidedly damp.

"Can we skip the drawing part?"

"No cheating, beautiful." He tossed a pencil in my direction. "But if you don't get started, parts of my anatomy are going to explode, and you wouldn't want to be responsible for that, would you?"

I couldn't help giggling as I picked out one of my new sketchbooks. "Most definitely not. Now, lie back and smile."

He did, only my grin was wider, and with good reason. This was my new life, and I loved it.

EPILOGUE

"AIEEEEEE!" I LEAPT on the bed, tripped over a pile of clean laundry, and landed face-first in a pillow.

Joe's footsteps thundered up the stairs, the new stairs he'd spent two weeks building. "What's wrong?"

"Vár brought me another present. A rat this time." I pointed at the wardrobe in the far corner, another of Joe's projects. "It ran under there."

Yes, I know what I said about no more cats, but when we bought the dilapidated ex-farm in the country five months ago, she'd been living in one of the rickety outbuildings. A skinny tabby, I'd named her after the Norse goddess of contract, which seemed appropriate given how we ended up with the property, and she'd soon worked out where the bowls of food were in the main house. She was sweet as anything apart from her penchant for bringing me all manner of wildlife. Last week, I'd spent half an hour chasing a sparrow around the lounge, and a fortnight before, she'd left a slow worm in one of my slippers.

Joe grabbed a torch off his nightstand and stooped to look under the wardrobe. "It's only a mouse."

I resisted the urge to roll my eyes. "Tell me again why we moved to the country."

"So the neighbours don't call the police when you scream my name."

That made me grin insanely, but I still threw the pillow at him. "Can you take Mickey outside? Somewhere far, far away from the house?"

"Anything for you, beautiful."

"And quickly, because the guests are arriving in half an hour."

Joe paused to cup my cheek in one rough hand. Since he started renovating the house, he'd developed a few calluses, but I secretly loved how they felt against my skin when he ran his hands over my body. The burn of his stubble against my thighs drove me wild as well, but he'd shaved today, most likely because my parents were coming to see our new home for the first time.

"Don't panic, Catie. Everyone knows this place is a work in progress. Nobody's expecting it to be perfect."

I knew that, even if it wouldn't stop my mother from looking down her nose at everything. No, my nerves were due to the extra people I'd added to the guest list without Joe knowing, and I still didn't know how he'd react when they arrived. If they arrived. They said they'd come, but...

"Got it." Joe held up the shoe box he'd just evicted a pair of my LK Bennetts from right as the doorbell rang. "Come play hostess."

I peeped through the curtains and spotted Sonia's car parked outside, complete with Marie's miniskirt-clad backside pointing towards the sky as she rummaged in the boot—for what, I dreaded to imagine.

Voices sounded from downstairs as I hastily tugged on the grey cashmere jumper dress I'd never have dared to wear six months ago and checked my reflection in the mirror. I still had hips, and ass, and boobs, but my stomach was a lot flatter now and my thighs no longer jiggled as I walked. The transformation was partly due to the effort I'd put in helping Joe with the house, but more because of Sonia's love of Zumba. As she was making the effort to be nice, I'd felt obliged to accept when she invited me to join her for a class, dragging Marie along with us for moral support. Marie had soon stopped complaining when she set eyes on Fernando, the Spanish instructor whose Lycra shorts didn't leave much to the imagination. Apparently, his limited knowledge of English didn't hamper his performance in the bedroom. I'd taken to sticking my fingers in my ears when Marie started describing their exploits in excruciating detail. Andy who?

Anyway, the three of us went to a class after work every Monday and Wednesday, and the pounds had slowly shifted, aided by Joe's love of cooking healthy meals, which stopped me dialling for all my food.

Down in the dining room, Sonia, Reggie, and Becky were hanging a "Happy Housewarming" banner between two wall lights while Miguel arranged a bouquet of flowers and Marie sprinkled sparkly confetti between the plates of nibbles I'd laid out on the table.

When she saw me, she dropped the packet and rushed over to give me a hug. "This place looks amazing! I can't believe what you've done to it in such a short time."

"What Joe's done, you mean."

We'd only lasted another week back at Heron Court. Even though Joe had filled in all the holes in the ceiling and the police had cleared the loft of its creepy cameras, my skin crawled constantly from the feel of Dane's eyes on me even though he was currently serving a two-year prison sentence for his sick games. Thankfully, the staff back at the Reuben Hotel had been only too happy to accommodate us again. We'd been prepared for a long stay, but Joe had surprised me the first weekend by taking me on a proper date to a lovely country pub, and on the way back to London, we'd happened to drive past White Horse Farm.

I'd never seriously entertained the idea of living in the country, but I wanted to move to a house rather than another flat, and something about the place made me curious. Maybe it was the crooked wooden gate, or the twisted tree next to the drive, or simply the way it needed some TLC to bring it back to life, just like Joe.

Whatever it was, when I glanced across at him, I knew he'd had the same thought, and no words were needed for him to jerk the wheel and head down the pot-holed drive.

I wish I could say it was love at first sight, but when my mouth dropped open, it was from horror rather than delight. The inside looked like something out of a seventies horror movie—ugly wallpaper, threadbare carpet, and a few pieces of ancient furniture. Oh, and did I mention the dust? Well, there was lots of it, a grey layer covering everything with a mess of scuffed footprints trailing through every room.

But when I looked at Joe, his eyes were gleaming.

"What do you think?" I asked him. I almost didn't want to know.

"I think that with some work, this would be the perfect place to bring our children up. How about you?"

Damn my ovaries. They overrode all rational thought with images of mini-Joes running through the woods beyond the tumbledown barn, laughing in delight as their father picked them up, one in each arm, and carried them into the house. And if we had a little girl, there'd be room for the pony I'd always begged my parents for but never got.

So, while there were a million reasons I should have come up with for vetoing the idea of buying a glorified shack, all that came out was, "Is there a train station nearby? You know, to get to work."

Google soon showed us that there was, a mere five-minute drive away on the main line into Paddington. And that was how, just three weeks later, Paul Campbell's money bought us the keys to the kind of house that until then had only existed in my nightmares. Not that we needed a key—one decent shove and the front door would probably have fallen right off its hinges.

But Joe halved his shifts at the gym and set up a carpenter's bench in the barn, and we moved in a month after that. Room by room, he transformed the place with me helping at weekends, and what do you know? I kind of enjoyed the whole DIY thing. Plus, if Joe bent me over that carpenter's bench one more time, the little Joes might be arriving sooner than we planned.

"We've brought champagne," Sonia called, snapping me out of my thoughts. "It's in the car, but it needs to go in the fridge."

I gave her a hug, and Marie too, rolling my eyes at the sight of her barely contained breasts. She'd finally succeeded in dragging me to the underwear exhibition at the V&A, where she'd discovered the magic of corsets, and now she had a whole collection. Today's was hot pink with black lace around the edges.

"And I also got you a little housewarming gift," she said, shoving a carrier bag into my hands.

"You shouldn't have." I peered in the top, and my eyebrows knitted. "A microphone? Karaoke?"

"That's a Bodywand plug-in massager. They're one of our best sellers."

Sonia leaned over and rummaged around. "And a butt plug? Lucky girl."

I didn't bother to stifle my groan. "No, you *really* shouldn't have."

A voice came from the doorway. "Did I interrupt something?"

I looked up to see one of Joe's colleagues from the gym grinning at us. Could this get any more embarrassing?

"Uh, I don't suppose you could forget you ever heard that part?"

Marie pulled out another packet. "Remote-control love egg?"

"Please, just put it away."

Sonia was still eyeing up Joe's friend. "Is that guy single?" she whispered.

"I think so."

She reached over and plucked the love egg from Marie's fingers. "Mind if I borrow this?"

Good grief. The poor guy wasn't going to know what hit him.

After I'd shoved Marie's bag of goodies right to the back of the wardrobe, the party went more smoothly. Even when my mother arrived and tutted about the champagne being Marks and Spencer's own brand rather than Veuve Clicquot, it didn't dampen my mood, although I almost choked on a mini-bruschetta when I realised the confetti Marie had sprinkled all over the table was, in fact, tiny multi-coloured boobs. Luckily, my mother was too vain to wear her glasses most of the time and the other guests saw the funny side. Even my father, and when I spied him creeping outside with a large wine glass and a bottle of red, I snuck out after him.

"Joe left a couple of seats for us in the barn," I said, and Daddy spun around.

"I didn't mean for you to leave your own party."

"Oh, I'm quite happy to escape for a few minutes. Like father, like daughter, right?"

A slow smile spread across Daddy's face. "Then lead the way."

We settled into a pair of old Ercol easy chairs Joe had rescued from the living room when we moved in, and I borrowed Daddy's glass and took a long swallow. Half an hour until my surprise guests arrived. Would Joe still be speaking to me by the end of the evening?

"Your young chap's done wonders with this place," Daddy said.

"He has. I can hardly believe it's the same house, but I'm still not sure Mother likes it."

"Your mother's fondness for any property is directly proportional to its distance from Harvey Nichols."

I choked out a laugh. "I'd never thought of it that way before, but you're right." Sod it. I took a swig from the bottle. "Has she said anything more about Joe?"

"Reckon he won her over at that last cocktail party. I overheard Margaret Pringle-Hines complimenting his derriere, and your mother didn't disagree with her. And she hasn't complained about his lack of title or choice of career since then."

"That's good, I think."

"Makes for an easy life. So, will I be walking you down the aisle soon?"

I spat a mouthful of Châteauneuf-du-Pape across the dirt floor. "Daddy!"

He shrugged, unrepentant. "Mark my words, it's going to happen. I've seen the way he looks at you." Daddy nodded at his wine. "Better not drink too much of this or I won't fit into my tuxedo."

"Can we change the subject?"

He gave me a "go ahead" gesture.

"Have you tried any interesting cases lately?" I asked.

When in doubt, talk about work. But even as Daddy chattered on about his latest fraud case—all hypotheticals, of course—I began to wonder whether there was any truth in his words. Catie Streeter? Catie and Joe Streeter-Jenkins. If Joe asked, I already knew what my answer would be.

***

The party was in full swing when a nondescript Ford estate car trundled along the driveway, and I slipped outside to welcome the family I'd only ever spoken to on the phone. Reggie had helped me to find the Colliers, but even after he tracked down their phone number, I'd spent two weeks plucking up the courage to make the call.

I'd been speaking to them for over a month now, mainly mid-morning conversations with Mrs. Collier as I sucked down my second or third coffee of the day, and she'd painted a very different picture of past events from the one in Joe's head.

"Joe almost died trying to save our Craig, and then we let him down so badly with Freya."

"What happened? If you don't mind me asking? I know this must be difficult to talk about, and I'm so sorry you lost your son."

"I'll miss Craig until my dying breath, but he was doing the job he loved until the end. What really hurts is that we lost Joe too."

"He thinks he's the one who let you down."

Her gasp was loud and painful. "What? Why?"

"Because of Craig. He said you wouldn't look at him when he went to the funeral."

A long pause followed. "We didn't know what to say to him. His sister almost died in our care. We should have been the ones to pick up the pieces from that incident, but with Craig... Freya took second place. I'm ashamed to admit that, and we'll never forgive ourselves for it."

"It sounds like she's on the mend now, though?"

"Thanks to her brother."

Oh, what a mess. Everyone blaming themselves when all they really wanted was to be a family again. The love in Mrs. Collier's voice was evident when she spoke about Joe, and I knew how much he cared for them.

"Do you think you could come to visit us? To talk to him?" I asked.

"I'm not sure that's a good idea. What if he gets upset? The last thing we want is to disrupt the new life you've built together."

"You won't disrupt anything. I promise. Joe would love to see you again."

"Are you sure?"

"I'm positive."

Only now that four virtual strangers were climbing out of the car at White Horse Farm, I wasn't quite so certain about Joe's reaction as I'd made out. Mrs. Collier grasped her husband's arm, looking as nervous as I felt, while Freya did the same with Hannah. I didn't need an introduction to those two—it was obvious which of the girls was Joe's sister because she shared so many of his features. The dark blonde hair, blue eyes, strong jaw. I kept my fingers crossed she hadn't inherited his stubborn streak too.

"Hi, I'm Cate. Would you like to—"

Mrs. Collier's eyes went wide as she looked past me, and I knew instinctively who she'd seen.

"What the...?" Joe asked from behind.

"Uh, surprise?"

Oops.

Joe took a few steps closer, and I could feel the nervous energy radiating from him, a crackling charge that made every one of my hairs stand up.

"Why are they here?" he asked me.

My mouth gaped open, but no words came out. Despite the amount of time I'd spent planning this, I really hadn't thought it through, had I?

But Freya stepped forward before I could make a difficult situation worse.

"We missed you," she said. "All of us. We all missed you."

A tear rolled from her eye, and she sniffled. Then Joe was there to wipe her cheeks dry. He hugged Freya, and then Hannah hugged both of them, and it only took a second for Mr. and Mrs. Collier to join in as well.

Awww. This moment was even sweeter than when Joe's bank balance had swelled to seven figures courtesy of Paul Campbell, even if it did leave me standing around like a spare part. At least, until Joe held out a hand and beckoned me into the huddle.

"Meet my family," he whispered to me. Then to the Colliers: "Meet my everything."

Dammit, now I was crying too, and I'd made the mistake of putting on mascara for the party. Smart, Cate. Really smart.

Freya must have read my mind because she flashed a smile as she rubbed at the mess around her own eyes. "Don't worry. We'll tell everyone the demented panda look is fashionable."

Joe leaned in close, his lips brushing my earlobe. "Panda or not, I've never loved you more than I do right now."

***

And the surprises kept coming. Most of the guests had trickled out when I heard the *click* of Mother's heels on the wooden floor behind me.

"I must say, Catherine, that I wasn't expecting much from this place. When your father told me you were buying a tumbledown farm..." She wrinkled her nose in distaste. "But it's actually quite nice."

"Sorry?"

"Yes, your Joseph has done a good job on the repairs."

My mother had just paid us a compliment? I should have taped the moment for posterity.

"Close your mouth, dear. It's uncouth to stand

around with it hanging open. Anyway, your father and I would like to buy you both a housewarming present. One of my friends has just opened up a new interior design showroom. Vintage with a modern twist, and I think that style would suit this place perfectly. Are you free next weekend?"

Mother was offering to help me decorate? She may have had her faults, plenty of them, but one thing she did know was style. I'd always been secretly jealous of her ability to make any room beautiful, a trait I hadn't managed to inherit.

"I'm free Saturday and Sunday." Even if I weren't, I'd have rearranged my diary.

"Wonderful. We'll start by heading to Shoreditch, and we can have lunch together too. Send me the measurements for each room, and I'll sketch out some ideas."

"Okay."

I leaned forward to give her a hug, but she dipped her head to air-kiss me instead.

"Goodnight, Catherine."

"Night, Mum."

***

I let out a quiet squeal later when Joe picked me up and carried me over the threshold into our bedroom. Mr. and Mrs. Collier had driven back to Oxfordshire, but Freya and Hannah were sharing the only habitable spare room. Joe needed to spend some time with his sister, who seemed to come as a pair with her best friend, and we'd agreed to drop them back home tomorrow evening.

"Ready to open a bottle of champagne?" I asked, relieved beyond measure that today had gone according to my loosely formed plan.

"No, I'm ready to open a case of champagne, pour it into the bath, and fuck you in it. That's how I feel right now."

Hmm...champagne sex. Bubbles. "There's an off-licence a mile down the road."

"It can wait. Getting you naked can't."

I reached for his belt buckle, but before I could it get it undone, he pressed a finger to my lips.

"Wait. I have a question for you first."

"Does it involve my favourite position or chocolate? Because if it's anything else, I'm not sure I want to hear it."

"Are you sure?"

He dropped to one knee in front of me, and my heart lurched. No. Surely he couldn't be about to—

"Catie, I fell for your sweet smile the first moment I laid eyes on you, and now I can't imagine life without you in it. Would you do me the honour of becoming my wife?"

My heart began tap-dancing while my vagina rolled out the red carpet, and I sank to the floor beside him. "Nothing would make me happier."

He kissed me long and deep, arms wrapped around my waist, holding me tight as our tongues tangled. I was well and truly breathless by the time he pulled back.

"I'll buy you a ring tomorrow, and I reckon we should upgrade that crate of champagne to a truckload."

"Or a swimming pool."

"We can afford a swimming pool now if you want one."

"Maybe just a hot tub. I have a feeling you'll give me enough exercise in the bedroom."

Joe's eyes glittered as he reached for the buttons on my blouse. "It's a promise."

What Comes Next?

If you enjoy romantic comedies, why not try my Trouble series? It starts with *Trouble in Paradise*...

When Callie Shawcross's fiancé jilts her days before the wedding, her best friend insists a relaxing break in the sleepy Egyptian town of Fidda Hilal is just what she needs to escape her disastrous love life.

The sun is shining and the locals seem friendly, even if the hotel staff do seem intent on playing matchmaker. But what better way to get over a broken heart than with a holiday fling? A sexy stranger who even makes a wetsuit look hot provides the answer, but is he all that he seems?

A series of mysterious disappearances leave Callie hunting for answers, and during her frantic search she finds it's not only the town that has secrets. Will she end up wishing she'd stayed at home with the ice cream?

Find out more here: www.elise-noble.com/trouble-in-paradise

Or if you're in the mood for some darker humour, you can find out more about the mysterious Diamond in *Pitch Black*, the first book in my Blackwood Security series.

Even a Diamond can be shattered...

After the owner of a security company is murdered, his sharp-edged wife goes on the run. Forced to abandon everything she holds dear - her home, her friends, her job in special ops - she builds a new life for herself in England. As Ashlyn Hale, she meets Luke, a handsome local who makes her realise just how lonely she is.

Yet, even in the sleepy village of Lower Foxford, the dark side of life dogs Diamond's trail when the unthinkable strikes. Forced out of hiding, she races against time to save those she cares about. But is it too little, too late?

Find out more here: www.elise-noble.com/pitch-black

If you enjoyed *Life*, please consider leaving a review.

For an author, every review is incredibly important. Not only do they make us feel warm and fuzzy inside, readers consider them when making their decision whether or not to buy a book. Even a line saying you enjoyed the book or what your favourite part was helps a lot.

Want to Stalk Me?

For updates on my new releases, giveaways, and other random stuff, you can sign up for my newsletter on my website:
www.elise-noble.com

Facebook:
www.facebook.com/EliseNobleAuthor

Twitter: @EliseANoble

Instagram: @elise_noble

If you're on social media, you may also like to join Team Blackwood for exclusive giveaways, sneak previews, and book-related chat. Be the first to find out about new stories, and you might even see your name or one of your ideas make it into print!

And if you'd like to read my books for FREE, you can also find details of how to join my advance review team.

Would you like to join Team Blackwood?

www.elise-noble.com/team-blackwood

END-OF-BOOK STUFF

My inspiration for this story was an article I read on the BBC news site about a homeless model. A bit of a silver fox. He'd shower in the gym in the mornings, go to a photoshoot, then sleep under a tarpaulin on a roof at night. Kind of intriguing, because nobody realised.

And Joe vs. Dane? In so many books, the heroine has to choose between the boy next door and a sexy prick. The nice, normal guy's supposed to win out, right? Well, I decided to make my hot guy genuinely nice, with no mercurial moods or spanky paddles in sight. And just for fun, I made my "normal" guy off-the-charts freaky.

I think many women have a little bit of Cate in them—I know I do. Calm and confident in some areas of life, totally inept in others. I wanted to show that difficulties can be overcome. Plus I got to channel her while doodling pictures of male body parts. Oh, the hardship.

The property angle came after I audited a couple of property developers for my day job, learning about the joys of planning disputes and ransom strips. I'd get in the car and spend an hour driving to Oxfordshire every morning, and by the time those accounts got signed, this story had taken root in my head. It's not what I normally write, but it was fun to take a break from all

Emmy's shooting. Although I couldn't resist having her make a cameo in *Life*—did you spot her?

As always, I couldn't have published this book without my wonderful team. I said to Abi that I wanted a cover with a naked dude on it, but we couldn't show his actual bum or Amazon and Facebook would get pissed, and she came up with this awesome cover that I love so much. And "in my head Joe looks like Chris Hemsworth" translated into the little sketch on the back cover :) Thanks also to Nikki for editing—I won't forget to capitalise Tube next time. And to my beta readers: Quenby, Nikita, Jessica, Stacia, Musi, Lina, Terri, Helen, Renata, and Harka. And finally, thank you to the proofreaders who hunt down my typos at the end —Emma, John, and Dominique.

OTHER BOOKS BY ELISE NOBLE

The Blackwood Security Series
For the Love of Animals (Nate & Carmen - prequel)
Black is My Heart (Diamond & Snow - prequel)
Pitch Black
Into the Black
Forever Black
Gold Rush
Gray is My Heart
Neon (novella)
Out of the Blue
Ultraviolet
Glitter (novella)
Red Alert
White Hot
Sphere (novella)
The Scarlet Affair
Spirit (novella)
Quicksilver
The Girl with the Emerald Ring
Red After Dark
When the Shadows Fall
Pretties in Pink (TBA)

The Blackwood Elements Series
Oxygen

Lithium
Carbon
Rhodium
Platinum
Lead
Copper
Bronze
Nickel
Hydrogen (2021)

The Blackwood UK Series
Joker in the Pack
Cherry on Top (novella)
Roses are Dead
Shallow Graves
Indigo Rain
Pass the Parcel (TBA)

Baldwin's Shore
Dirty Little Secrets (2021)
Secrets, Lies, and Family Ties (2021)
Buried Secrets (2021)

Blackwood Casefiles
Stolen Hearts
Burning Love (TBA)

Blackstone House
Hard Lines (TBA)
Hard Tide (TBA)

The Electi Series
Cursed

Spooked
Possessed
Demented
Judged

The Planes Series
A Vampire in Vegas
A Devil in the Dark (TBA)

The Trouble Series
Trouble in Paradise
Nothing but Trouble
24 Hours of Trouble

Standalone
Life
Coco du Ciel (2021)
Twisted (short stories)
A Very Happy Christmas (novella)

Books with clean versions available (no swearing and no on-the-page sex)
Pitch Black
Into the Black
Forever Black
Gold Rush
Gray is My Heart

Audiobooks
Black is My Heart (Diamond & Snow - prequel)
Pitch Black
Into the Black
Forever Black

Gold Rush
Gray is My Heart
Neon (novella)